PARABELLUM

Stars of Avalon

~*Book I*~

STARS OF AVALON SERIES

Melissa L McGuire

~ PARABELLUM ~

<u>Dedication</u>

In loving memory of a great man,
who always taught me to follow my dream's.
Forever in my heart.
You will always be, my greatest hero.

~* Dad *~

Acknowledgments

Firstly, I would like to give thanks first and foremost to my amazing partner Adam.
Your continuing support over the years has helped guide me to be the woman I am today. Through some of the hardest trials that we have faced together, you have stood strong and steadfast in the face of adversity. Shown patience and understanding when things grew dark and tiresome. Always believing in my own potential when I was struggling to see it within myself. You truly are my best friend, for that I love you. To Christine Gardner at Editing Indies, thank you for the amazing cover art. You truly are a woman of many talents. To my friends and family who have supported me at various times throughout the years, always saying encouraging words to help me stay on track. To all of you I say from the bottom of my heart.
~Thank you.

~Melissa. L McGuire
I didn't fail. I just postponed my success

Prologue

30 B.C
A hidden location
in the forest of the glass house mountains.

The lanterns burned brightly lighting our path.
The slaves slashed away at the thick
undergrowth.
"Faster. The full moon is almost upon us."
screeched the priest.
Emaciated arms reached high above the slave's
heads, with every upward swing of their
machete's.
Starvation and scurvy had taken many of my
men, as we journeyed across the ocean.
All that remained where a few slaves, two of my
royal guard and the priest.
Suddenly, a scream echoed from deep in the
darkness up ahead. A hurry of footsteps came
towards us. The priest turned to the guards,
hurriedly telling them to go investigate.
Fear was plain on every one's faces. Wide eyes
frantically searched the darkness around us. The

sound of running water echoed from a nearby stream. Cicadas sung high and mighty through the trees in a deafening chorus.

The guards came back, speaking hurriedly to the priest. He nodded as the men spoke.

Leaving the men behind he Strode towards me, speaking softly as he came closer to where I stood. "My Pharaoh, we have found the hidden doorway."

"Show me."

On wards we pressed, making our way through the group of slaves. Trekking further into the thick rain forest.

"Here is where he disappeared." Stammered one of the slaves.

His eyes showed fear as he took steady, cautious steps back to where our small group was now gathered.

The guards extended their burning torches towards the darkness that now settled deeper in around us.

"There's nothing but undergrowth." One of the guard's exclaimed. Impatience clear in his voice. He squinted, trying to see any signs that would point us in the right direction.

"Your wrong. Look! There. Just beyond those

trees." The priest pointed to a large gum tree that stood ten feet from where we were gathered.

The thick trunk shone white, as though beckoning for us to find it.

My patience was at its final thread, I would not miss this opportunity. Turning to the slaves behind me. I snatched a torch.

I moved the torch over the surface of the tree. The air seemed to move with its light as though absorbing the flames energy.

Extending my hand towards the trunk I touched the air. My hand disappeared until only my forearm was visible.

"Come! Bring the sarcophagus." I called over my shoulder.

With a renewed feeling of purpose, I fearlessly plunged myself forwards disappearing inside the hidden doorway. I could feel my foot touch solid ground.

I shielded my face trying to protect my eyes from the sudden light. I lost my grip on the torch, and it fell. There was a splash as the torch hit the water.

What was only a distant trickling of water outside, was now a deafening river inside. The sound caused my ears to ache, as the noise reverberated off the walls. The current flowed downwards below an overhanging rock beside my feet. I quickly stepped aside, away from the steep drop.

There was a crunching sound beneath my feet. I was still struggling to see, blinking rapidly as my eyes adjusted to the light.

Squinting I could see leaves laying thick and drying. As my eyes adjusted, I could see more clearly. Leaves lay scattered like pebbles covering the cavern floor.

I looked around, studying my surroundings. Immediately I could see where the light was coming from.

Stone walls encrusted in millions of gemstones, surrounded the cavern. They extended upwards reaching up to a naturally formed sky light in the cave's ceiling.

Flowing through the large opening, was the silver white light of the full moon.

Moonlight cascaded down helping to illuminate the enormous cave. The gemstones where absorbing the moonlight, creating a transfer of otherworldly energy.

I watched in awe as the energy was projected

outwards, giving the illusion that the wall was alive. The air felt tight, as though the energy would burn you alive if you stood too close. It was that energy that was lighting our path in the grand cave.

My 'seemingly' lost slave now stood in front of me. A look of both awe and fear consumed his frail hollowed face. I moved two steps forward towards him, but he didn't seem to notice.

His fear came off him in thick waves, in an almost suffocating aura. I placed a hand firmly on his bony shoulder.

He jumped violently, whimpering and mumbling. Using my power, I willed him with my own energy to gaze up into my eyes. I projected my will for him to remain calm. To be still, and at peace.

I browsed through his memories, capturing snippets of his favorite moments.

I channeled those happy, joyous emotions. Filling his mind with the possibility of safety, promises of warmth and comfort.

The fear he held was suddenly released, in one long staggered breath. His breathing quickly returned to normal. I slowly removed my hand from his shoulder.

I ushered him to move further into the cavern, making room for the priest and my two guards as they materialized through the doorway.

The priest was holding a thick book, bound in elephant skin. Which held all the incantations we needed to complete the ritual.

I moved my attention back to the cave. Three white trees stood in a circle. Their branches had grown entwined over time as though they were gently holding hands. Leaves crunched loudly as I walked forward towards the trees.

In the center of the rough circle stood a jagged blue translucent stone. Its dominating beauty stood three meters out of the ground. I walked around its base, my fingers tracing its cool rough exterior. Energy vibrated through my fingers, I stopped at the base, and craned my neck skyward.

Looking up through the skylight to the glowing full moon above.

The moonlight fell over me, and while I basked in its eternal glory, I knew this was the place. I stepped back from the stone, the energy vanishing as quickly as it came. I couldn't help but feel as though a part of me hungered for more. I wanted to hold that energy, let it consume me. I turned to my priest, forcing myself to brush the feeling aside.

"Go. hurry! The time is upon us." I ordered him. My voice sounded harsh as it echoed through the cave

The moonlight sat inches from the stone's surface. A few more heartbeats and it would be in position. I felt my body go numb with anticipation and excitement. I could see the light moving ever closer. as the moon rose higher above us. We had only minutes to recite the incantation and complete the ritual, before the moon engulfed the stone entirely. My heart beat harder in my chest making my throat form a tight, metallic tasting ball of anxiety.

My slave had gone to join the others as they made their way through the doorway. I could see him offering up the last bit of strength that he had to help the other slaves carry the heavy sarcophagus. The priest was speaking so fast I could barely make out the words.

He turned suddenly, grabbing one of the slaves by the front of his throat.

"*STOP!*" I screamed.

The priest looked at me, bewilderment in his eyes. I grabbed my slave as he lay the sarcophagus at my feet, pulling him by his arm towards the priest.

"It must be this one." I said, as I threw my slave down on the floor.

My slave looked at me, a pleading look in his eyes.

I turned my cold gaze back to him. I projected my thoughts into his mind.

"*I know what you are, I have always known, that is why I chose you.*"

A smirk filled his face. He responded wordlessly, his voice echoing painfully through my mind. As though just his voice alone would tear me apart. It felt as though his presence was too big inside such a confined space.

"*Then so be it. Take me if you must but know this. You will not get what you desire. Cleopatra. For though my mortal body will be killed. It is only a shell.*"

Our eyes locked together in a silent battle of will, only to be broken by the Guards. As they commanded the slaves to move the sarcophagus beside the stone. They shuffled

forwards, struggling from exhaustion. The
sarcophagus made a heavy thud as it was placed
down haphazardly onto the ground.
The slaves removed the lid, exposing my beloved
Antony wrapped inside. The smell of palm wine
mingled with cinnamon and myrrh filled the air.
The guards picked up my slave. and guided him
into the sarcophagus.
They held him tightly as his body sat straddled
directly on Antony's mummified remains.
The chanting grew louder, the priest stepped
forward holding the ceremonial knife. My slave
now an unwilling sacrifice, made sure his eyes
remained locked on mine. The priest drew blood
from his wrist the knife making a clean cut
against his skin in one quick slash. The priest
rubbed it over the face of the stone. Leaving a
trail of thick red blood, illuminated on the
surface. Still the slave did not take his heavy gaze
from me.
Then without warning the priest lurched
forward, stabbing deep into his chest piercing his
heart.
His body jerked back, before going limp and
weightless.
He slid forwards, as the priest withdrew his

blood-soaked blade. Blood stained his hands in a sticky red coating. The now lifeless body lay covering Antony's remains entirely.

Blood ran in a steady flow from his chest in thick crimson streaks, coating Antony's bandages and dying them a deep red.

Moonlight engulfed the entire stone now, the priests rapid speaking suddenly stopped. Time itself came to a standstill.

The sound of water that was deafening only moments before slowed. The air itself became heavy.

There was a tremor beneath my feet as the stone moved up, further out of the ground. Its highest tip now protruding out of the skylight.

My guards took a step backwards, but the priest and I held our ground.

The trees creaked loudly.

I turned to see their branches entwining tightly around each other, forming a thick in penetrable wall that rose high above the ground.

Inside the stone I could make out a dark shape trapped deep inside. I pressed my hand to the stone and was shocked to feel it was now ice cold.

I knew what I had to do. "Bring me the chest." I

said to my guard, who gave a sharp nod.

He turned with purpose on his heels, striding like a tower of bulky strength, to a slave that stood clutching my gold chest.

His hands clasped the sides tightly as if it where the last thing on earth. My guard loomed over him before giving a grunt, then snatching it impatiently from the slave.

He strode back and stood beside me clutching the heavy gold chest.

It was emblazoned with the two enormous wings of Isis, which sat on either side of a raised golden scarab beetle.

The guard held the chest out to me. I gently spread apart the golden wings exposing a small circle. A perfect fit for my engraved peridot ring. Closing my hand into a fist, I pressed my ring, into the circle and turned it clockwise. A large click sounded as the lock mechanism was released.

Opening the chest I looked inside with admiration at the gemstone necklace that I had created.

I ran my fingers across the stones, their smooth cold surface felt like silk in my hands. I gently lifted the heavy gold amulet from where it lay

placing it on my chest. The priest came to me,
helping to do up the clasp.
The moment it touched my skin the five
gemstones sprang to life. Their colour's flared
brightly in a blaze of brilliant light.
The priest once again began to read. As the
slaves brung forth a woven basket.
I opened the lid and reached inside. An asp
snake slid itself around my wrist, winding its way
around my arm. Hissing, the snake revealed its
fangs. Two sharp needles protrude from inside
its mouth. Walking to the stone I placed the
snake onto my breast, just below the amulet.
Without hesitation it strikes me. I try to place it
back into the basket, fumbling as my hands and
arms go numb. This time there is no antidote for
the poison, as the snakes venom begins to burn
through my veins.
I let go of the Asp and watch as it slithers away, a
feeling of calm overwhelms me as I lay a hand
upon Antony's sarcophagus.
I have a moment of reflection. To think of how
the gods have rewarded us, aided our escape
from Octavian. So that we may be together for
eternity.
There is a deafening crack as the stone splits in

two. A thick Grey cloud of smoke oozes out from the inside, quickly filling the circle with a thick fog.

A voice fills the cavern, with an echoing bellow. I can't understand the words, the language sounds foreign. It is a language that I have never heard before. I Cleopatra who knows so much of the world, am now fearful.

I look at where the priest stands, still reciting from the sacred book. He looks at me true fear fills his eyes, then suddenly it is silent.

A silence so deafening that it presses on your eardrums, threatening to rupture them. A high-pitched buzzing now remains.

I look up, my vision is wavering as the poison takes its hold. A woman now walks forward through the fog. Pausing for a moment to lay a hand on the strange man's arm before, kneeling down in front of me to where I am huddled. Vulnerable and dying I struggle to keep my eyes focused.

Her skin is the colour of honeycomb, her eyes are large and green like emeralds. Her hair is as silver as the moon, flowing down in long waves covering her naked body.

She reaches out her hand, while smiling gently

at me.

We hold hand's as she rises, helping me to my feet. The woman is a true goddess, she is over six feet tall. Yet she smiles gently at us as she towers above us all.

"Thank you." she says smiling.

"your sacrifice has freed us." I look past her to the other man. A second man has appeared from the fog. I try to look at them.

One man has hair as golden as the sun. He has the same large piercing, emerald green eyes as the woman. Complete with matching honeycomb skin. The other man however is just as tall, but his hair is as black as night, his skin so pale it glows silver in the moonlight.

It is this man who walks further forwards, placing a gentle hand on the woman's shoulder she moves back to stand beside the other man. Now beside one another I can see that they are identical, the only difference in them both is that they are of a different sex. They both hold the same facial structure, a femininity that made the woman look ethereal makes the man look stunning in contrast.

I can see the woman lay a hand upon her swollen stomach. Surprised I realize that she is with child.

My attention was bought back to the man who now stood in front of me.

I craned my neck back to look at him properly. His hair was long and looked soft and weightless. As it hung in waves around his arms. His eyes where a brilliant blue that matched the Lapis Lazuli stone, I had on my amulet.

It was as though the gemstone itself was born from these very eyes. The man smiled at me with thick red lips, the colour of blood. He looked into my eyes, and for a moment it was as though all my troubles were suspended, in a sea of calm ocean. Waves appeared in front of me. It felt as though each wave was a memory, that crashed down onto the next wave below. Before it evaporated entirely as though it was never really there at all.

A voice echoed inside my head. It whispered across the sea of those waves, filling me with an emptiness.

"Your memories hold great pain. Tell me, what do you wish for? let me grant you your true heart's desire."

"For Antony and I to be laid to rest together. To be free from our bodies being violated." I replied, my throat now dry and my voice now choked from the poison that now consumed me. "Then so it is done." The world around me grew small, and darkness enveloped me. I could feel my life slipping away like a veil being lifted. My body became weightless as I floated upwards. The moons light shone brightly across my body as I floated through the air. I looked down towards the ground at my crumpled body which now lay sprawled on the cave floor. I did not feel scared, I felt free.

I looked skywards towards the heavens and felt a pull as if the stars themselves where beckoning too me. I smiled, as the moonlight grew brighter before my eyes, I knew I would be transported home, to live in peace with my beloved Antony. Among the gods forever.

Chapter One

our voices caress the dreams, of those too blind to see us.
Ghostly figures of shadow, that glide through time and space
we always will be, just as we have always been.
The smokeless fire that is, the great almighty D'Jiin.

Trapped and suffocating. I was engulfed entirely, by
what appeared to be an impenetrable darkness.
I was lost to the deafening silence of the abyss. A
space that existed without the confines of time or
space.
This place had no name. Or none that anyone alive
today could tell you. It was only known as, the in
between.
How did I get here? who was I? I didn't even know, let
alone remember. Somehow as I floated silently, the
questions seemed important.
I was confused not knowing, which was the right
question, or even which was supposed to be
answered. I felt paralyzed. Suspended in this never
ending space, unable to scream or move.
Strangely I didn't feel afraid. I knew somewhere in

the back of my mind, that I should be scared, possibly screaming out with fear. Yet the more I tried to hold onto that thought, the more it felt as though   these emotions seemed irrelevant.

Each emotion melted away, only to be replaced by an empty calmness.

My body relaxed before a sudden feeling of warmth crept over me.

The empty-ness that surrounded me entwined itself around me.

Then without warning the darkness lifted. I was left falling through space before finally being grounded. The sudden atmospheric change made my bones ache in pain as though the air itself where made of led.

I was left lying in a brightly lit hallway, my face pressed against the cool floor.

The sudden change of light burnt my eyes, as I struggled to stand.

Feeling began to return to my body. I turned my head and tried to focus on my surrounds. The glare was slowly fading from my eyes. I blinked rapidly trying to rid my eyes of the white dots that scattered my vision.

A long banister stretched out before me. White limestone shone brightly in the glare of the sun.

I Followed the line of pillars that stretched like giants into the air. There was a staircase, roughly carved in the stone. That wound upwards. Through the structure. I moved my gaze towards an upstairs landing. There on the stone wall where pictures of god like creatures, painted in intricate detail.

I had never been here before and yet, I had a feeling deep inside me of belonging. As though this place was where I was supposed to be.

I stepped forward, leaning on the banister trying to center myself.

The rough stone felt cool under my palms.

'was I dreaming, was any of this real?' The thought barely had a chance to manifest before the screaming started.

From the deepest parts of the stone structure, a woman screamed in terror.

The scream was so blood curdling, my ears throbbed with the sound. My feet moved of their own accord towards the screams. Running and tripping slightly on the roughly carved steps, as I worked my way up to the upstairs landing.

Before I could think of what to do next, I was standing inside of a tiny round room.

Moonlight flowed brightly in through a tiny window which had been cut out from the stone wall. The silver moonlight illuminated the room, with its bright, white blue glow.

The center of the room held a bed. Beautiful hand carved pictures of Isis adorned it's base. I had a moment to think *'How beautiful.'* Before my attention was drawn to the woman who lay in pain on the bed. Her hands were bound together with coarse rope. Her wrists where rubbed red raw from struggling.

A giant sheet hid her body. Silver hair shone brightly in the moonlight, cascading down over her shoulders. The parts of her body that I could see where covered in henna tattoos and outlined in gold.

She looked at me with tear stained eyes. Our eyes locked onto one another and her screaming ceased. Her body which was struggling only moments before, now lay completely still.

I stepped towards her, never breaking her gaze. Her beautiful emerald green eyes looked straight through me. As though they were reaching into the depths of my very soul.

I felt no fear, only a sense of longing that I couldn't understand.

I took one last step forwards before kneeling down beside her. My knee pushed painfully into the cold stone floor.

I went to speak, when another scream escaped her lips. Her back bowed violently as she screamed in pain towards the ceiling.

Her body lifted in a contorted spastic way that seemed unnatural.

As I sat beside the woman, I did not feel fear. Then before my eyes, I saw the darkness form. It wound like a deep wisping shadow, slowly rising up from within her throat. It grew like a cloud of bodiless

smoke, enveloping the screaming woman. It grew
until there was nothing left to physically see. The only
thing that stayed where the screams. Now muffled
behind the veil of darkness, that hung like a deep
cloud. Without thinking I reached into that darkness.
I held my hand firmly around the woman's, squeezing
her hand ever so slightly.
The darkness seemed to retreat, as though it had
been stung. The woman looked at me, with a gaze full
of strength that had not been there moments before.
As she held my gaze she whispered, her voice hoarse
from screaming. "Sophia. Never forget who you are
my child. For the Gods, will forever hold you in their
heart. Only you and Juliana are worthy to harness its
true power. Help guide us back into the light."
Then giving one last scream, there was abrupt
silence. I sat on the stone floor, still holding the
woman's hand.
The darkness shifted above me, I tried to look within
the darkness. There seemed to be a stirring coming
from within the giant mass itself. The sound of
clicking grew louder, reverberating off the stone
walls, in a deafening chorus.
The darkness broke. Releasing thousands of shiny
black scarabs, that rained down like a wave covering
the bed.
I let go, scrambling backwards. My back hit the wall
behind me. I stared in horror as the scarab's clawed
their way over the woman's now lifeless body. Some

entering through her mouth and ears. While others wasted no time creating small pockets to burrow their way inside. Lumps formed behind her skin as they crawled their way deep into her body. As they fed, blood trickled down her skin, soaking the sheets. I sat paralysed with fear. Unable to move, as the darkness seemed to reach outward towards the blood-soaked body. It's cold silent shadow quickly consumed the entire bed.

I awoke in a cold sweat. 'It was just a dream. Dear god. It was only a dream.'

I kept telling myself repeatedly as I sat in the darkness of my room.

I couldn't shake the horrible feeling of horror that the images in my dream had left behind.

Shaking and swatting at myself as the image of the scarabs made my skin crawl.

I turned on the bedside lamp, wanting to chase away the darkness. I pressed the button on my phone to check the time, it was 3am.

Sighing I flicked the lamp off then I rolled back over, trying to think of something pleasant to fall back asleep with. Eventually, I fell into a dreamless sleep. Wrapped in the warmth and safety of my bed.

Chapter Two

It was four thirty in the morning when I got the call. The metallic ringing piercing through my sleep fogged mind, waking me up. My hand fumbled in the darkness, trying to grab a hold of my mobile.

'Success!'

I thought as I grasped the phone.

Squinting I checked the caller I.D. It was Jones, my partner on the force. We were both senior detectives with the Criminal Investigations unit. Grudgingly I answered, lazily putting the phone to my ear.

"Hello." I said, my voice sounding groggy with sleep.

"Jules, wake up!" He yelled down the phone. I gave a grunt, jerking the phone away from my ear drum.

"Come on, we have orders to go to a crime scene." Pressed Jones.

"Okay. Okay. I'm up.' I replied. my voice was a little clearer... Just.

Still holding my phone, I rolled myself one handed out of the comfort of my warm bed. I still felt groggy and struggling from lack of sleep. I dragged my feet like a zombie half walking, half stumbling. Over to where I had thrown my dressing gown onto the floor the night before.

"Hang on a second." I said grumpily into the phone.

I put my mobile phone down on the bed, so that I had both hands free to put my dressing gown on. The room was freezing, which was no surprise for our cold July weather.

We were getting average overnight temperatures of minus two degrees Celsius.

The warmth of the added layer of clothes made me feel a little better. Really what I needed was a hot shower, immediately followed by a good hot cup of coffee. Just the thing to help my tired brain wake up enough to think.

"Are you still there?" I asked, as I picked up the phone. I managed to walk semi normally out of the bedroom, groggily making my way down the hallway. I stole a peek into Sophia's room, I had heard her call out in her sleep a few hours ago. She was sleeping soundly with her blankets wrapped around her like a cocoon. I closed the door gently and continued down the hall into the kitchen.

"Yes. Are you up?" He asked, sounding impatient.

"Yes, unfortunately." I yawned, as I flicked the button on the kettle.

Then I turned and walked back down the hall to the bathroom.

"Jules, there's been a double homicide down south side. I'm sending the details to your phone now."

"Okay, I'll be there in the next half an hour."

We hung up. I quickly stripped off my clothes and turned the shower on. I had mastered the art of the three-minute shower. Increasing drought across Australia had made water conservation everyone's responsibility. Washing my hair would have to wait Not that it was an issue. My hair was so frizzy and curly anyway. That I could just throw it up in a bun and no-one would know the difference.

Thankfully my chocolate brown hair was dark enough to hide the fuzz that some people had when their hair had been conditioned.

For me, that was just a regular hair day.

After rushing through the shower, I wrote a note for my housemate who, was also my best friend and my sister.

Sophia and I had been inseparable since birth. We were inseparable then, and a lot hadn't changed as adults either. We are the only family that each of us have. We never really knew any of our extended family. Our parents both died when we were sixteen. For weeks there was no sign of them, and the police had no leads. Then almost a month after their disappearance, they found their remains. Left deep in the thick bush land of the Kosciusko National Park. Hikers had stumbled across their bodies as they scaled down the ravine. They found the people responsible shortly after.

Two brothers who were seriously screwed up in the head and not very smart.

The crime scene was every forensic investigator's jackpot. There was forensic evidence left everywhere. My mother had defensive wounds as well as skin fragments lodged under her fingernails. They had kidnapped them, held them prisoner on their farm for weeks.

When the police went to the farm to arrest them, the brothers had never tried to run. One of the brothers was found in a coma. The other was in the dining room, barricaded under the dining table. Screaming about, shadow people. And how they were coming for all of us.

When they got him to the police station, he refused to say a word. Then later that night, he hung himself in his cell.

The police didn't tell us a whole lot at the time because we were under eighteen years of age.

But that didn't matter because Sophia knew, she always knows.

Her precognitive abilities jumped forward after that. I would spend many nights holding her while she wept uncontrollably, from the horrors that plagued her dreams.

Being a teen was hard enough, without having to deal with the loss of both parents. Let alone seeing, the details of what they had both gone through.

Sophia and I were put into foster care. Many people would often comment, that we were both each other's perfect opposite.

My dark hair and blue eyes were a perfect contrast to Sophia's emerald green eyes and pale blonde hair. My skin was pale while Sophia's was a perfect olive brown.

When I was nineteen, I decided to become a police officer. It took me two years after joining the police force, to pick up the courage to find the file on my parent's case and read it. I still don't sleep properly after seeing the gruesome images. It really made me feel more sympathetic towards what Sophia endures. Here we are twelve years later, I'm still in the Police Force and still loving my job.

Today wasn't just supposed to be my day off, it was also Sophia and my thirty first birthday. Did I mention before that we are twin's? Pretty neat huh'. Sophia and I were supposed to go to the movies today, unfortunately it would have to be postponed.

I know that Sophia will understand, she respects my commitment to my work.

I have always had a job first attitude which is probably why I haven't had a serious relationship. Most men can't deal with the dedication I show to my work. Guess its intimidating or whatever the gurus of women's rights are preaching these days.

Frankly I don't have the time to date, or the time it takes to sustain a relationship. I didn't become a detective by sitting around all day.

It takes serious dedication and commitment, to become a detective within the Criminal Investigations unit. I would be lying if I said that Sophia's visions hadn't helped me. They have helped me solve a lot of crimes over the years. Some however, have left her scarred. I have been there to help her back to sleep on those nights that she has seen horrific things. Truth is, that some scars run too deep to heal. I left a note for Sophia beside the kettle. Then, after double checking that I had my uniform looking neat and tidy, my badge, my I.D, belt and vest I grudgingly left my apartment. I checked my watch it was 4:50am.

I lived in the southside of our not so big city. A modest sized apartment in the thriving shopping hub. Putting it at only a three-minute brisk walk to the station and twelve minutes' drive away from the crime scene. Though in honesty, most places in our city where a max travel time of 40 minutes, provided you didn't leave at 8am or 5pm and hit peak hour on the parkway, you were pretty much guaranteed a reasonably straight run from one side of the city to the other.

The cool air hit my cheeks and with it the familiar smell that always signaled that dawn was about to break. I could see the faintest glimmer of light trying to break through, ready to chase away the night. I yawned and rubbed my eyes 'err' I let out a groan. I needed more sleep; five hours just wasn't enough after finishing a double shift. With a sigh I sat in my car and shoved the keys into the ignition.

Chapter Three

My gut tightened as I pulled into the usually quiet
cul-de-sac, where police and forensic vehicles lined
the street on both sides.
Red and blue lights illuminated the houses. Helping
to chase away the long shadows that the old
streetlamps could not penetrate on their own.
The lighting made it look as though every house had
Christmas lights on.
I knew then, that this was no ordinary crime scene.
Not when there where these many police involved.
I parked in the last available space and quickly
hopped out. I startled as I accidentally closed my car
door too hard.
Sending a great boom of sound echoing through the
street. If you have ever had to work on minimal sleep,
you will understand that every light and sound can be
almost nauseating. As every one of your senses is in
overdrive. The lights hurt, any loud noises make you
startle, and I could feel a headache forming behind
my eyes.
Shaking it off, I walked briskly up the sloped street

towards the large two-story home that dominated the very end.

I paused as I got halfway up, a group of officers were stationed outside trying to keep the neighbours back. A temporary fence had been erected running the full length of the yard. It had been covered in thick white plastic sheeting that held the same blue and white design as the crime scene tape.

Mission one. Is to always protect the crime scene from being contaminated. Secondly. For the general public to stay clear for their own safety and to not contaminate the area. While the forensic team and the criminal investigative team finished doing their jobs.

The fence would stay there until our investigation of the scene and possibly the whole investigation if necessary, was concluded.

The forensic team was busy collecting evidence. They were covered top to toe in their Personal Protective gear. Dressed in blue coveralls, Long gloves, scrubs, safety glasses and masks.

'It looks like a scene from a Hollywood movie, how bad is this crime scene?' I wondered to myself.

Police where manning the front of the house trying to persuade the nosy neighbors that everything was under control. They had their hands full trying to persuade the neighbours, to leave and let us do our jobs. Jones had informed me already that constable Gray oversaw protecting and maintaining the crime scene.

I was given a silent nod of approval to go through the barrier by Constable Gray, who was among one of three officers at the front of the barrier.

Before I could enter the crime scene, my attention was drawn behind me to a reporting van that had pulled up. The van was from the local television station. The side door opened and out hopped a thin blonde woman.

"Shit." I cursed under my breath, recovering quickly I looked at Constable Gray.

"Looks like you boys have your hands full." I smiled, as I looked out at twelve concerned faces.

He turned to look at the news van, then back to me. "She's all your's detective, that's way too much woman for me to handle."

I rolled my eyes as I walked behind him and through a small opening in the fence.

"Tell her nothing Gray. No matter how many times she pushes you for info. We can deal with her later."

Gray nodded and smiled. "Yes Ma'am."

He replied trying to lighten the mood. His smile then quickly faded leaving him looking very firm and serious.

He turned to the other officer working beside him and passed on the message.

I walked across the front lawn. The early morning frost crunching loudly under my boots. I made my way straight towards my partner who stood waiting for me next to a tent, that had been set up outside the front door.

Jones had been my partner now for three years. We first met when we studied at the police academy together and he was moved to the Criminal unit three years ago. After a drug bust had gone wrong up North.

We don't talk about it much. His old partner Drew was shot in the Femoral artery during the bust.

Thanks to Jones' quick thinking he lived. He hates Jones and blames him for cutting his career short by about thirty years.

The truth is that Jones was left with a difficult choice, to either move Drew so he could put pressure on his wound so he wouldn't bleed out until the Ambulance arrived. Or leave him and watch him bleed out within minutes.

I don't blame the guy really; I'd be pissed too.

But I wouldn't hate Jones, especially when he saved the guy's life.

But hey that's just me. I guess some people are just pessimists at heart.

I personally, pride myself at being the glass is always half full kind of girl. Drew may be out of the active side of the force and instead stuck working behind a computer in the communications department. But... he can walk thanks to the twelve months he spent in the rehabilitation clinic.

Jones received the Commissioner's Commendation

award for Conspicuous Conduct. Which no doubt
angered Drew even more.

Jones is a bit of an introvert when it comes to talking
about 'feelings'. But hey, what guy isn't. He is
however a straight up kind of guy. If you ask him a
direct question you will get a straightforward and
direct answer. Just don't expect any lengthy
explanations or elaborations, especially if he doesn't
want or feel it's needed to give one.

I giggled quietly to myself at the thought of that.
Jones watched me cross the lawn, I could see he was
concerned.

I quickly wiped the smirk off my face, his dark
eyebrows where creased in a frown making the rest
of his expression seem very tense.

Jones was a big bulk of a man, not fat, just very broad
in the shoulders and well built.

Like most tall people he had a slight hunch as though
he was trying to disguise how tall he was. Or perhaps
it was from years of crouching through doorways.

They never seem to make them tall enough anymore.
I pictured an old English home with high ceilings and
generous doorways. That would be the perfect home
for Jones. Jones had a very square jaw line which was
exaggerated by his piercing dark brown eyes, and
equally dark brown hair.

If you were to compare his brown hair to mine, Jones'
would definitely be at least two tones darker, putting
it at almost true black.

If you saw him on the street you wouldn't be blamed for feeling slightly intimidated. Seeing him in his police uniform only accentuated his domineering appearance. It gave Jones that cool don't mess with me facade. In another life, he would have made the perfect bad guy.

He nodded a greeting to me.

"Hey Jules, Happy Birthday I'm glad you could make it here so quickly. I only just arrived a couple of minutes before you did."

There was no impatience in his voice now, like there had been on the phone. I watched as he eyed the house, and I got the distinct feeling that he had been stalling "Hey." I replied. Snapping his attention back.

"I waited for you to arrive before I went in. How are you feeling?" He seemed to shake off whatever he was thinking or feeling, or both for that matter. I pretended I hadn't noticed.

"I could definitely use a cup of coffee." I answered with a slight smile. Jones returned my smile and nodded in agreement.

"I second that! Shall we go in?"

Jones made it sound more like a statement than a question, as he gestured for me to go in first.

Whatever we were about to go into, Jones seemed just as spooked as I was.

"Age before beauty." I said jokingly.

"Heck of a way to be spending your birthday Jules."

"Yeah well, you can buy me coffee when were done."

"Deal." He replied giving me a pat on the back. We stepped inside the tent.

"Welcome to hell." Said Constable Smith, successfully startling us both as we came through the tent door. He was there to greet us, as we entered. Smith was also dressed top to toe in blue protective wear. "I hope neither of you have eaten yet, because it's not pretty."

My gut suddenly felt as though it held a large ball of led. Guess it's just as well I skipped that coffee then.

"Here. You need to get dressed." Smith gestured towards a rack that held full length blue coveralls. There was a table set up beside it with gloves, scrubs, masks and protective glasses.

We got dressed, then we followed Smith through the second opening.

This led through to the front door of the house. We all stood in the entryway of the two storey family home.

A large staircase dominated the entry hall.

Just then, a younger looking forensic specialist, who I had never seen before came rushing down the stairs. He was dressed top to toe in PPE. The poor bloke was trying to move as quickly as he could. I could see his I.D tag bobbing up and down as he stumbled in his haste to get out as quickly as he could.

Ripping off his mask as he came rushing towards us, we could see he looked quite grey. Jones and I side stepped quickly out of his way to let him past, as he flailed his arms wildly signaling for us to move. We moved aside as he ran out into the front yard, where we could hear him throwing up outside.

One of the Crime scene specialists called down to us from upstairs.

"Did he make it outside?"

I recognised the voice straight away before I saw the face. Some people's voices were unmistakable.

A husky voice that carried with minimal effort. I had a moment to think, 'that has got to be Dr Anderson.' Then she came down the stairs. Why does she have such a deep gruff voice you might ask? Well the answer is cigarettes. Dr Anderson was a smoker and a heavy one at that, years of smoking had made the fifty-year-old woman's voice sound hoarse and gravelly.

Smith stood with his now blue foot resting on the bottom step and he leaned his arm on the stair banister as he replied.

"Yeah, he's outside feeding the roses."

"Good, the last thing we need is to have contaminated evidence." Said Dr Anderson.

"Detectives, it's good to see you again. Shame it can't be under better circumstances. I'm ready for you to come upstairs, but make sure you are all in full Personal Protective Gear. It's a god damned mess up here!" She said shaking her head.

"No problem, we are all suited up." replied Smith.

Dr Anderson looked us up and down nodding to each

of us.

"Good you'll need your goggles, masks and gloves on before you enter the room." With that she turned quickly and walked back upstairs.

"So, what have we got?" I asked. As constable Smith directed the rest of us to follow Dr Anderson up the stairs. "We've got two murders. One male, mid-fifties. The other one female. Who appears to be in her late fortie's. Both were found in their bed. There is no evidence to suggest that there was a struggle. However, both victims were fully conscious before they died. Both have sustained what appears to be multiple injuries. We can't pinpoint the exact cause of death yet, but..." He paused shifting his gaze uneasily towards the stairs.

"But what?" I asked, getting a little impatient.

"Were not sure exactly. Well... It's just that it's weird." He stopped at the bottom of the stairs and turned to me. His facial expression showing a lot of frown lines.

"Weird how?" I asked.

"I think you need to see this for yourself." He responded.

Motioning us towards the bedroom door. He stood aside to let me pass. I walked up the stairs feeling each foot getting heavier and heavier with each step that I took. A knot had formed in my stomach as I reached the top.

Pausing for a second I took a deep breath, then I followed the line of officers towards the far bedroom.

At the doorway one of the constables stopped me from going any farther.

"I'm sorry, I just wanted to tell you before you go in there. It's a bad one Jules."

His voice sounded muffled through his face mask.

I nodded then took a deep breath before I walked in. I was still in the doorway when I froze. I gasped at what I saw. It made my head spin. I grasped the door frame and tried to center myself. Feeling slightly stable I removed my hand. Big mistake, my glove peeled away from the wooden frame like sticky tape, threatening to tear my glove to threads. Sticky red blood clung the palm of my blue gloves, making them a turn a deep shade of purple.I stormed out of the room and lent against the stair banister. I held my eyes closed tightly as I slowly tried to regulate my breathing.

'I will not have a panic attack.' I promised myself silently as I repeated it over and over in my head. I tried to steady my breathing, so I didn't throw up. When I felt calmer, I stood up straight and slowly opened my eyes. I waited a few moments so that I could pull myself together. Then like the trooper that I am I walked back into the horror scene that was

awaiting me, to finish doing my job.

Chapter Four

It was like nothing that I had ever seen before. In the twelve years I had been on the job, I had been exposed to a lot of crime scenes. It just came with the territory. But this was different. It was like something that had been taken directly out of a horror film. There was blood everywhere. It was sprayed crimson on the walls, over the carpet. Even the windows where stained. It looked as though someone had come in here with a thick bristled brush, to coat the glass with a coagulated coat of bright crimson paint. Small spotted patches of the once pale blue paint showed through in small areas around the room, like a dalmatian with a bad hair day. Except this was fifty shades of wrong, on so many levels.

The ceiling was the strangest part. It was completely clear and untouched.

As though something had obstructed the spray. Sending the pool of blood to projectile outwards leaving the entire ceiling clean.

Then laying smack bang in the middle of it all, lay the two victims. The killer had stripped their chests.

Leaving them void of everything including their skin.
Both of their rib cages laying white, glistening and
completely exposed.

Both victims had been hollowed out, stripped bare of
all their internal organs. What lay before me was
nothing more than two hollow carcasses. From the
waist up and the neck down, the whole center torso
was in complete disarray.

In all this horror, that wasn't even the worst part. The
worst part for me was that both of the victims were
just lying there, blankly staring up at the ceiling.
Completely void of any expression on their faces. It
was eerie to see all this mayhem surrounding the
room, and with the couple lying there just looking,
well...Peaceful.

My head began to spin, I needed air and fast!

As I pushed my way outside, I felt my chest tighten
and a lump rose in the back of my throat. The cold
morning air hit me as I barged my way out of the tent
entrance. Stumbling, I reached the side of the front
yard just in time to throw up into the rose bushes.
Jones came up behind me, presumably to offer some
kind of moral support. Wrong again.

"Better out than in, there Jules." He joked as he
patted me on the back.

"Very funny." I said spitting the last of the bial from
my mouth, that came up and out like a burning hot
wave of acid. Standing slowly, still not trusting my
stomach I turned gingerly around to face Jones' now

smiling face.

"So, how about that coffee?" He asked cheerily.

"Yeah, why not." I replied, shrugging my shoulders.

"So... Round two Jules?"

"No way! I think I'll be right sticking to just crime scene photos, thanks." He laughed, as he walked towards the waiting sergeants.

"Come on let's head back to the station, before anyone sees the mess you have left. Right beside the young guns remains. Which if you ask me looks suspiciously like, rice bubbles."

With that, I turned back to the rose bush and went for round two.

Chapter Five

As I stand in a tower with no doors or life
I look through a window to my dark world below.
My world was over run, by the power of hate.
I could have ruled but now, it's too late.

Earlier at 6:00am that morning

I awoke to the melodic sound of my mobile phone alarm going off.
Groggily I rolled over and ran my finger across the touch screen to switch it off.
Rolling back over I lay on my back looking up at the ceiling for a minute, Procrastination at its best.
'what a horrible dream.' I thought to myself. Giving a small shiver as I remembered the beetles falling onto the woman's body and eating her from the inside out.
'God it felt so real.'
Shaking the thought away I rolled over, flicking the blankets off. Grudgingly I sat up and sat heavily on the edge of the bed, I was still so tired.
Grabbing my thick dressing gown off the end of my bed, I walked lazily into the kitchen to make myself a

coffee.

A note sat on the counter beside the kettle, it was from Jules. Jules and I shared our apartment.

We had been best friends, sisters and each other's support for most of our lives. We are more like best friends than sisters. I can't remember a single time that we have had a fight, or harboured bad feelings towards each other.

Jules is the only person in the world who knows about my visions.

They started after our parents were murdered. I can remember at sixteen, waking up in a cold sweat one night after dreaming of a gruesome murder.

Jules comforted me until I fell back asleep. In the morning we saw on the news that a man had been burnt alive inside his house with his five-year-old son. After a rival biker gang had used him to send a message.

That was the moment that Jules decided that when she finished college that she was going to join the police force.

Jules has always credited much of her career success to my visions. Which have helped her solve many heinous crimes over the last twelve years.

Today was one of the rare days, that Jules actually has time off. Our plan was to go to the movie's after my morning lecture, to celebrate our birthday. Part two of our favourite Stephen King movie, remake was just released and its all we had been talking about for months.

However, looking at the note Jules had written for me it looks like that plan would have to be postponed. I stood looking at the little yellow post- it note stuck to the kettle.

Dear Soph,
got a call from Jones
going to have to postpone
PS: call me later
love Jules xx

That was one thing I always admired about Jules. The forceful, unselfish dedication she consistently gave to her work. It was one of the reasons that she is, where she is today. Working alongside the best criminal investigators in the Criminal Investigations unit. Where she has been for the last two years.
Jules had been given an award at the age of thirty, for her ten years of diligent and ethical service.
An award that had secured her place in the Criminal unit, and the resounding respect from her team.
The copper and Nickel medal hold's the sovereign crown, the nemesis eagle and the NSW State badge. It hangs from a symbolic five blue striped ribbon both dark blue and light blue, which pays homage to the states uniform.
Jules' name is inscribed on the reverse of the medal. I smiled to myself, as I flicked the switch on the kettle.

I was so proud of Jules, she unlike me always
followed through with everything she set her mind
to.
I on the other hand, I have never finished anything I
had started in my life.
I always felt like an outsider looking in, never truly
feeling as though I had found my purpose in life. It
was one of the reasons why at the age of thirty-two I
was still at Uni doing a degree. After our parents had
been killed when Jules and I where sixteen.
I had combined my inheritance with Jules', and we
had purchased this apartment when we turned
eighteen.
It wasn't until that moment that I truly understood
Jules' pain. The fact that she had endured not one
but two tragic deaths simultaneously in her life and
against all odds. Had continued to push forwards in
life and succeed. That in itself was a true testament
to her inner will. I on the other hand had always
considered her opposite I wasn't so strong willed or
focused.
The added stress of losing both parents
simultaneously had propelled my mental health into
a chaotic downward spiral. Jules had always been so
patient, even when everyone else had long left us to
our own devices. Isn't it funny how a family death can
bring such a circus of relatives crawling out of the
woodwork?
Only to disappear as quickly as they came. Once the

funeral proceedings have finished and the real grief
begins. No one seems to check in anymore.
A few days after we said our final goodbyes to our
family, that was when it started.
I crumbled, my visions grew worse and more
demanding. I saw so many psychiatrists, physiologists
and counsellors. Who all diagnosed me and treated
me for post-traumatic stress disorder, grief, loss and
behavioural therapy.
Now I'm only just getting back on my feet. Last night,
was the first night in two years that I had, had a
dream. The anti-psychotic medication and the mood
stabilisers had kept it at bay for years. I was so close
to graduating; this was my final semester. I only had
three months to go and I was done with my arts
degree. I can't fail, I'm too close. Jules would be so
disappointed in me. After my last mental relapse, I
created a mantra for myself which I recite every day.
'I didn't fail, I just postponed my success.' I recited it
in my head now, breathing slowly I felt it help to push
away the thoughts of self-doubt. I knew that when I
got to the lecture today that none of these feelings
would matter anymore. They were completely false I
knew I was doing well, and I knew that Jules was
proud of me. With that thought I made my coffee,
then went to get ready for uni.

Chapter Six

Dr Farez Amiri stood on the stage in the lecture hall.
He was an Archaeologist from Egypt, invited here to
our University as a guest lecturer.

He was the first guest lecturer in a while to not only,
have a full theater. But to be surrounded completely
by a captive audience.

The lecture theatre was silent, no one was bored or
falling asleep.

No phones in sight, every single student was
completely engaged in the presentation hanging on
to his every word. Eagerly awaiting what was going to
happen next.

I looked back at the stage. Dr Amari's assistant was
sitting at a fold out table on a laptop computer, which
was located at the side of the auditorium.

He was in charge of the slide show that was being
presented behind Dr Amiri, on the big pull-down
screen.

The slideshow was of pictures that he had taken from
the new Archaeology site at Alexandria. The pictures
showed the excavations they had just uncovered. The

new findings were just a little way out from the main archaeological site which was located near the Mediterranean Sea.

The next slide showed a digital photo taken of an ancient scroll made of papyrus. The worn scroll showed a picture painted, of what appeared to be a massive necklace. It was presented proudly around the neck of Queen Cleopatra. The unique necklace held five large gemstones, that looked as heavy as they were big.

Dr Amiri pointed to the screen behind him.

"The scroll that you see on the screen before you is an old papyrus scroll that was found buried in a tomb below the temple ruins."

"This ancient temple known as *Taposiris Magna,* is believed to be where Queen Cleopatra went, to be closer to her gods. Isis and Osiris."

The screen changed to a new image. This one showed a piece of Papyrus with Hieroglyphs covering the entire scroll.

"This is the reverse side of the scroll. Here you can see, that the entire piece of papyrus is covered in hieroglyphs. It is a detailed telling of the amulet itself; the translation tells a story. It says;"

"The Amulet is an amazing source of power. It gives the wearer the divine ability to not only store their own spare energy, but also gives the wearer the ability to harness, and absorb energy, from other

beings."

His voice boomed through the theater, there was a unanimous 'ooh' from the students. Dr Amiri continued.
"Storing the power within its five great gemstones, the amulet can regenerate power for its owner for an unimaginable period of time."
He paused, looking out at the eager faces of his audience. I froze as his gaze fell to me.
He looked straight at me as if studying me.
I shifted my weight uncomfortably, trying to look away, in the hope that he, would do the same. My heart sank as I looked back to find that he hadn't.
Without shifting his gaze, he continued speaking.
"There is no concrete record of what the amulet is actually made of, only speculation. Based upon what we know of the ancient Egyptians, it has been suggested that the Amulet is made of *electrum,* which consists of gold, copper and silver." His voice was a little softer now, forcing the people around me to lean forward in their seats.
"This speculation and guess work is, in large part due to the fact that the amulet itself was created and then sadly lost. No other record of the amulet has ever been found. Though it is believed that Queen Cleopatra designed the Amulet herself. This theory is furthermore made more convincing, by the signature left on the bottom of this piece of papyrus. As you

can see it holds the Hieroglyphic imprint of the royal scribe." The imprint was of a serpent eating its own tail.

"This symbol is known as the *Ouroboros,* it is the oldest symbol in Alchemy, and in lamens terms, it depicts eternity as well as the alchemists well known search for immortality.

Given Cleopatra's well known devotion to the gods, as well as her affinity with magic and alchemy. We can only fantasise, over what her sole purpose was for creating this amulet."

He gave a small smile at me as he turned and strode to the other side of the stage.

"It is here that we are currently searching for the lost tomb of Cleopatra and her beloved King Antony.

We know that Cleopatra experimented with different poisons, using her prisoners as test subjects. Some vials of her home made poisons where recovered intact.

Laboratory testing has concluded that the contents were not only different poison's, but more mysteriously, they contained hallucinogens. As well as the ingredients for anti-venom."

Dr Amiri fell silent as another image flicked onto the screen. The image was of flames.

Within the flames where two eyes staring out. Dr Amiri took in a deep breath before continuing. "Who knows what this is?"

he bellowed excitedly as he pointed at the screen

behind him. No one answered.

He strode across the stage, his long legs making short work of it as he moved in just a few steps to where I sat.

"What's your name?" He gestured to me.

"Um." I stammered. "Sophia. My name is Sophia." I managed to spit out.

I was slightly taken aback at such a simple question. "Do you know what this picture is of, Sophia?" I paused looking at the screen.

I felt as though I knew the answer, but the answer seemed stupid and clearly incorrect. As though he read my thoughts. Dr Amiri gave me an encouraging smile.

"No answer is stupid Sophia. Please go on, have a guess."

"Okay..." I replied sounding uncertain. "It reminds me of a picture I once saw of a Dj*inn* or as we know it as, a *Genie.*"

"YES!" He bellowed. Now full of excitement. "Here we see a painting of a Dj*inn.*"

Sophia. Can you tell me anything more about the ancient Dj*inn*?"

I paused before answering. "The Dj*inn* are from the middle east. They are also known as *spirits of smokeless fire.* They don't grant wishes, nor do they live inside bottles or lamps."

Dr Amiri seemed impressed by my answer. He turned to his assistant who gave a nod of acknowledgement.

"Yes, that is correct Sophia. The Dj*inn* are believed to live among us on a separate plain to humans. Separated by only a thin veil. Therefore, they cannot be seen by the naked eye. This painting was also recovered from *Taposiris Magna*. The Dj*inn* are recorded in the Quran and tales of their existence are widely known throughout both the Middle East, and the rest of the world.

It is written that the Dj*inn,* like humans. Have free will and so choose to either be good or bad. Many conspiracy theorists believe that they are responsible for our supposed Ghost sightings, alien abductions and mysterious disappearances. While others believe that you can magically bind a Dj*inn* to an object and therefore control it."

He gave a dramatic pause for a moment scanning the crowd as he continued.

"Yet the question must be asked. Why a being such as this, has been recorded in almost every ancient civilisation around the world? The name. The physical appearance. They all may differ slightly. Yet each story, has all the same depictions of these ancient magical and albeit immensely powerful beings.

One theory on this is that Queen Cleopatra herself, In her obsession with immortality. Set out on a perilous quest across the ocean. A quest to find the perfect hidden burial site, for her and Antony to lay to rest. Her mission was to find somewhere that would never be disturbed by grave robbers. One which could imbue her identity as a goddess.

For Cleopatra this was vital to how they would spend their afterlife. The Egyptians believed that, before you could go through to the afterlife. You must first go to the *Land of testing.*

Cleopatra was obsessed with the tale of Osiris and Isis. The tale tells of, Osiris' brother Seth. Chopping his body into pieces and throwing them to the crocodiles in the Nile River.

Isis retrieved every piece of Osiris' body. In fear that he would not be able to continue to the afterlife until he had been given a proper embalming and burial. Therefore, remaining trapped in the land of testing forever.

Cleopatra feared that if their graves were disturbed, then they too would be lost in the land of testing for eternity. It is for this very reason that, the most famous of all the Queens of Egypt, and her beloved King Antony have been lost for thousands of years."

He paused staring out at the eager students.

"Could Cleopatra have created this Amulet to bind a Dj*inn* within it and use it to help her hide their bodies? Or is there something more to the five gemstones than meets the eye? That is one story archaeologists like to tell around the campfire."

Dr Amiri gave a small giggle, the class also giggled.

"Regardless of why the Amulet was created. It's whereabouts, like Cleopatra herself. Remains one of the world's biggest, Archaeology mysteries of all time.

To this day the whereabouts of their tomb remains a mystery that many are eager to solve. Thank you all for your time. I hope that this has stirred up some excitement, for that inner archaeologist in you."

The theater erupted in cheer as all the students praised Dr Amiri for his presentation.

Dr Amiri stayed to allow students to ask him questions.

The rest of the lecture theater became full of noise as the students packed up their belongings to head to their next class.

I began putting my notebook and pen away in my bag, just as I got up to leave, I heard my name.

"Excuse me Sophia!" I turned towards the call.

Dr Amiri's assistant came hurrying toward me.

"Yes?" I replied. Making it sound like more of a question rather than a statement.

"I am very sorry to bother you; I know you must have other places to be. Please, just a minute of your time. Dr Amiri would like to speak with you."

"Really?" I replied. Unable to hide the surprise in my voice.

"What could he possibly want with me?" I asked narrowing my eyes in suspicion.

"Please it is nothing to worry about. Have a seat, Dr Amiri will be with you soon."

He gestured to where I was sitting throughout the presentation.

I nodded and took a seat. Feeling both bewildered
and curious.

I sat back down in my chair and waited patiently. As
one by one, the students took turns to have a one on
one chat with Dr Amiri.

After about fifteen minutes, Dr Amiri politely excused
himself, then pretended to busy himself with his
assistant, while the students left the theater.

When the door closed for the last time, Dr Amiri and
his assistant stopped talking. Turning and walking
over to me he smiled. I stood politely as he extended
his hand out to me. "Sophia Helios, what a pleasure
to finally meet you."

"How do you know my name?" I asked. my heart
began beating faster. A mixture of surprise, curiosity
and deep suspicion overwhelmed me.

"Come." Said Dr Amiri. "I will answer all your
questions. I have much to discuss with you, and not
very much time."

Chapter Seven

I stood staring at Dr Amiri, waiting for him to give me more of an explanation. 'What could be so urgent, and what the heck did it have to do with me?' My thoughts started racing.

He took a deep breath before continuing. "I'm sorry Sophia, please let me explain." he motioned to the chairs and sat down, waiting patiently for me to do the same.

I sat, eager to find out what the hell was going on.

"Sophia, you and your sister Juliana are in extreme danger."

"What!" I exclaimed, standing abruptly. I was completely confused. My heart was pounding in my chest as I started to feel a combination of both fear and anger.

I knew that Jules' police work sometimes put her in dangerous situations but what the hell was going on.

"What are you talking about?"

"What Dr Amiri is trying to say Sophia, is that the murder investigation she has been working on these past six months is placing her and you in grave danger." Dr Amiri's assistant looked at me pleadingly to stay and listen.

I let out a long breath, trying to calm down.

"Ok, as crazy as this sound's I'm listening."

"My apologies Sophia, my name is Danny." he extended his hand, I took it shaking it softly, not putting much effort in at all.

"We have been trying to follow the path of recent killings that have taken place across the world over the past year. All the murders are the same and the police can't string them together.

Although we do know that it is the same killers."

What does that have to do with Jules and I being in danger?"

"It's complicated, it stems back to when Jules and yourself where teenagers when your parents were murdered." I shifted uncomfortably on my feet.

"Tell me Sophia, when did your visions start?"

Dr Amiri looked at me with a solid look.

"How?" I began to ask, but Dr Amiri put up his hand and stood.

His six-foot height towering over me as he came closer. I looked away towards Danny as I answered.

"They started the night that our parents went missing."

Dr Amiri sighed. Nodding quickly, he turned and walked back to the stage to collect his belongings. I stood dumfounded, millions of thoughts begun sweeping through my brain, in a mad attempt to peace all the information together. I could feel my arms go numb with the feeling of shock, as I struggled to hold back several emotions. I watched Dr Amiri madly grabbing papers off of the stage table and shoving them in his briefcase.

"We must go, immediately. We cannot linger here for long, they with find us."

"Who will find us!" I could feel the anger in the back of my throat like a little ball of fury. Good, anger I can comprehend. At least one thing was going my way at this moment.

"We must leave now; I will explain in the car. He reached towards my arm, I flicked it away from him. Glaring at him before I screeched.

"No, I am not leaving until you tell me what the Fuck is going on!" I screamed right in his face. There, I was angry and rightfully so. Before I could say another word, Danny stepped towards me and there was a sharp burning pain in my neck. The world swam as I collapsed to the floor.

Chapter Eight

We arrived back at the station just as the news was being reported on the radio. Double homicide rocks Canberra. I sighed heavily, turning to Jones. He shrugged, "You knew it was going to happen Jules, by not saying anything they are just creating a story instead."

"We need to organize a press release to calm the public before everyone starts freaking out." I replied.

"I couldn't agree more." a heavy deep voice said behind me making me jump.

"Don't be so jumpy Jules."

"Sorry Sarge, I'm running on empty."

"Here Birthday girl have a coffee." He handed me a hot cup of heaven. Jones gave me a small smile from behind his desk. Sneaky bastard must have said something on our way back.

"Have the photo's come through yet?" I asked wanting to change the subject.

"Yeah I'm just downloading the file now."

The great thing about modern technology is that now days you can snap photos and do a virtual tour. This means that every angle of a room is photographed using what's called a live shot and put together to give a full 360-degree visual video of the room. Real Estate agents have taken to using this for their house inspections and sales lists for homes. Once completed its electronically sent through E-mail. The files come straight through our system. Reducing waiting times and increasing productivity by hours. I pulled up a chair next to Jones and prepared myself for the gruesome images I was about to see.

There was something surreal about photos. It was as though a small part of your brain just clicked and said, 'Nope, not real just pretend.' Resulting in the ability to be able to see things more clearly, rather than trying to see everything when your face to face with the carnage in real life.

The video image loaded onto the screen, it showed the bed and the bodies. The clean expressionless faces of the victims laid staring blankly towards the ceiling.

The bed was soaked in their blood, the walls sticky and crimson.

The video moved around the room, showing the rest of the walls, the blue paint that once covered the room was coated now, with only small patches showing. The video turned towards the window, that was on the opposite wall at the front of the bed. There sitting just above the left cornice was a small circular black dome.

"Pause the video!" I said excited. "There, look in the

corner." I pointed at the black dome. Jumping up
from my chair I grabbed my phone, quickly scrolled
through my contacts list and found constable Grays
mobile. Clicking on the little phone icon I waited
impatiently for him to answer. After the fourth ring
he picked up.
"Jules, what can I help you with?"
"Gray. There's a surveillance camera in the bedroom,
you need to find the central recorder and bring it in
as evidence!" I said hurriedly, not wanting to waste
another precious second. I could hear the faint sound
of him walking then the phone made a crinkling
sound in my ear as he moved it across his vest.
"Hey, Smith get down here, we need to search for a
surveillance recorder."
He held the phone back up to his ear. "We will search
now; I'll call you as soon as we find it."
"Excellent, thank you."
with that I hung up and looked at Jones. Fingers
crossed something shows up on that tape coz at the
moment, it's the only lead we have."

Chapter Nine

I felt the world moving around me, as I came to I
could see that I was in the back seat of a car.
Dr Amiri sat beside me, I looked down wondering
why I couldn't move. My hands and ankles where zip
tied together. Fear coursed through me like pin pricks
running through my chest and arms.
Dr Amiri looked down at me. "Ah excellent your
awake, sorry we had to do that. As I said, time is not
our friend. Now I promised you an explanation." He
pulled a laptop out of its bag and sat it on his lap.
Turning it on, he waited patiently for it to start up.
"You might want to sit up and see this and I'm sorry
in advance as its pretty gruesome."
I shuffled upwards with great effort Dr Amiri put an
arm around my shoulders and pulled my up wards.
Finally, I was sitting upright, and facing the screen,
which was all black except for a little light that was
running around a circle in the centre to show it was
now loading.
The image on the screen was black and silver, as
though it was filmed using night vision. It was a

bedroom, the camera faced down from the ceiling, over the foot of a bed that dominated the centre of the room.

Two people lay seemingly asleep. Slowly a dark shadow seemed to grow across the top of the video covering what must have been the ceiling.

Out of nowhere, a part of the shadow came down to stand at the foot of the bed. The longer the shadow stood there the more substance it began to have.

The shadow moved in what appeared to be wisps of dark smoke. the person on the left of the bed sat up. It was a woman, her long hair brushing over her breasts in two long lines. The light filtering through the window below, illuminated her skin. An arm stretched out from the shadowy mass, giving a gesture with a shadowed hand as though it was silencing her.

The woman's body contorted. Her shoulders going outwards in an angle that just shouldn't be possible. Her face fell into an expression of calmness, her eyes held no emotion. Then without warning, blood began to come forth through her skin, like small pin pricks all across the top half of her body. The bleeding grew stronger streaming down her torso onto the sheets. Before the drops seemed to coagulate and began turning outwards in a stream which floated through the air. b Landing in splashes across the walls, in a sea of red.

The body beside her was now doing the same, I could

see the man's face held the same blankness.

When the blood began to stop pouring through the air the shadow reached forward with two arms and pushed himself inside the woman. Reaching inside her chest cavity, through the base of the sternum, just below their rib cage. He emerged seconds later with two large chunks, which disappeared into the dark smoke.

Then he repeated the same torment on the man. Afterwards he retreated then melded back into, the larger shadow that consumed the ceiling.

The darkness melted away silently leaving the ceiling as the only surface left bare in the room. My attention went back to the horror that lay on the bed, what was left where two corpses. If you could call them that. Rather it was two faces and a shining hollow rib cage lying in blood on the bed.

Both victims had their faces turned upwards, towards the ceiling and where completely untouched. Not one speck of blood stained their faces at all. And they both held the same calm expression. As though nothing had happened.

Dr Amiri closed his laptop. 'I'm sorry, I warned you that it was gruesome."

he looked at me, studying my face. Frown lines creased his forehead. "You aren't scared, are you?"

I wasn't sure how to answer that question, I was still trying to come to terms with what I just saw. That same shadow had appeared in my dreams last night.

Seeing it again shocked me but something in the back of my mind held me back from feeling scared.

It was as though a part of me knew, it was going to happen and yet, how was that even possible?

A thought popped into my mind. "When was this video taken, and more importantly, how is this video even on your laptop?"

After we heard on the police radio about the murder. Danny hacked into the victims Wi-Fi and downloaded the security footage onto my laptop. This murder happened at three am this morning." Replied Dr Amiri.

Danny shifted in the driver's seat. "The cops arrived on the scene fifteen minutes later. Apparently, they received an anonymous tip." His voice sounded sarcastic as if he knew more to the story.

Dr Amiri turned to me, studying my face. "Why do you seem so interested all of a sudden?" He asked, his voice sounding a little smug.

"Because, at 3am this morning, I was dreaming of that shadowy thing killing someone else."

Chapter Ten

The clock ticked loudly on the wall of the office. The silence inside the room was an uncomfortable one. I stood behind the desk, grasping the back of the leather chair.

Which sat behind an incredibly large handmade mahogany desk. It was so large, that to get it upstairs into the office it had taken five large strongly built men just to carry it up here.

Piece by piece it was carried. Carefully taken up the three flights of narrow winding stairs. The leather crinkled loudly in the silence of the room, as I squeezed the back of the chair in frustration. I clamped my jaw tightly as I let out a long, controlled breath. I closed my eyes, centering myself, counting calmly to five in my head. I had promised that I would not lose my control.

I had come too far to blow my chances now. I could feel the urge, the need, building inside of me. I gestured to my assistant.

"Bring him in. Let's get this over with."

I remained as neutral as possible. I could not show

any form of weakness to our prisoner. If he knew what I was, even that I where here. God's help us, if he knew what I was searching for, then all would be lost. The key to my plan's success rested on maintaining the element of surprise.

I could feel my body temperature rising, as I fought back the urge to lose control. Patience had never been my strong suit. I had devoured my fair share of Fey in my time for doing far less than the one I was about to see had done. There was a heavy creak, as the guards strode into the room and forcibly sat my prisoner into the chair, on the opposite side of my desk.

I stared across at the pitiful creature that sat sweating and trembling in fear. I composed myself, stepping gracefully around from behind my desk. I moved towards the male faerie that sat shaking before me. I leaned back, resting my backside on the front of the desk. My leather boots creaking as I crossed my legs. I was unarmed, but I had otherworldly weapons ready at hand if the need for them should arise.

I was hoping that we could avoid such a full-on confrontation. The meeting was supposed to remain calm, so as not to arouse suspicion. A lot was at stake, everything was riding on this moment.

The Fey where cunning, sneaky creatures. I did not believe for one moment that this creature, who possessed such great power was really frightened. It was all an act, a test of sorts. To see what my next move would be.

I had a moment of fear. Had he found out? I tried to shake the niggling thought that burrowed in the back of my mind. A jolt of fear ran up my spine, I pushed it away. No, there was no way he could know. I had been so careful to disguise my true form.

The male Faerie looked up into my eyes, I returned his gaze. Unflinching, I sat staring deep into his pale green eyes and showed no emotion.

Those piercing eyes had been my pride and joy once upon a time. Centuries had passed since I stared into those eyes with even a remote thought of the love, I once held for him. There was a time when his eyes seemed to hold the energy of the world in them. A green so deep that the greatest emeralds of the world could never compete. Now they lay empty, like a baron wasteland of the man he once was. I smiled, a friendly inviting smile, trying to relax my body. I was trying to appear as casual and inviting as possible. The moment I did that I could sense the tension leave his body, he took the bait, his body visibly relaxed. Lesser beings would have used magic and trickery to do what I did. It takes a stronger more intelligent being to use nothing more than body language and self-control. We were older, more cunning creatures. After being among humans for centuries and using them as vessels. We had become professionals at hiding in plain sight. All the while waiting patiently, plotting our return and learning about the world. I was the first to look away. Not out of discomfort, but rather playing coy. Appealing to his masculine side. He responded by leaning forward towards me in his chair. As though it was just two old friends. He knew the game; he was playing me.

'Not today, underling.' I said silently to myself. 'You're in my maze now little mouse.' I stood abruptly boldly walking with my back turned, trying to exude an air of naivety. I stopped when I reached the hutch that stood against the far wall, complete with an under-bar fridge. It had been custom made to match my desk. "Would you like a refreshment?"

I asked smiling as politely as I could muster. The male Faerie returned my smile. "Yes. thank you, I am quite parched."

I purposely turned with my back to him again. I grabbed a glass out from the cupboard in front of me. I knew that by turning my back on the Faerie it would help to keep this meeting on track. Usually turning your back on your enemy was a foolish mistake. In most cases this would be true. However. When dealing with older creatures such as Fairies, turning your back to them is a gesture of good faith. To them it is a compliment of sorts, it says. 'I know you can kill me where I stand, but I am showing you polite trust.' Due to their ancient codes of conduct, they will always return this show of trust with honour. Never the kind of creature to win a fight by being deceptive. Always killing a foe while looking them in the eye, unflinching and without mercy.

They believe without any reservations whatsoever, that when they do resort to violence and killing another being, that it is for just, and legitimate reasons. Therefore, the need to 'stab someone in the back', so to speak is gutless. The ancient forest folk strongly believe that by doing so, you are dishonoring yourself, your bloodline, and your elders. One of their many faults and the main reason I knew that I would come out victorious today.

Time has crippled the Fey, once a power to be reckoned with, now the Fey had taken to hiding in their forests between the realms. Steadily growing weaker every year, as the old ways of the ancient deities slowly fade from humanity. Descending instead into nothing more than myth and legend.

I reached into the fridge, retrieving my most prized possession. A simple crystal bottle that sat securely in a tailor made bottle holder. It was an ancient bottle of, *Water Vierg'e.* There it stood glowing luminescent. sparkling a crystal clear blue that appeared to glisten in the light of my office. The longer you stared into the tranquil blue water, it was as though a thousand tiny stars swam glistening inside.

Only the purest of waters run down through the *Mountains of Vierg'e,* and only the purest of souls, could ever capture its essence.

I turned, with the bottle in my hand. "Do you know, what this is?"

A look of astonishment sprung onto the Faerie's face.
I ignored him and pressed on.
"This is the purest of waters ever, to be found on this
Earth."
Legends tell of the Djinn prince of darkness, who
fought against the Djinn gods, to rescue the Faerie
princess of light.
The princess was kidnapped by the Djinn Queen,
imprisoned within a secret cave. She was hidden
within the tallest mountain peak, strongly warded to
prevent her from ever escaping. He vowed he would
not rest until he had rescued her from her prison.
When he won the battle against the queen, he faced
his final test. He set out to climb the perilous
mountain.
Wounded and bloody he reached the top of the
mountain. There he found his princess *Vierg'e.*
Unfortunately, he was too late to save her. The
queens magic had entombed her. She lay trapped for
eternity, inside a crystal so large only the tip
extended from the earth.
He collapsed helplessly at her feet crying out his tears
of anger and sadness as he felt defeated and
consumed with his grief.
He prayed to the gods to save them. So that they
could remain at peace together, living forever in
secret, away from the war of the two realms.
The Gods, seeing that their love and devotion to each
other was unbreakable. Wept tears of sadness, that

someone could destroy something so pure. Their
tears fell, soaking deep into the mountain's ice. The
God's gave the prince his wish. They shrouded the
cave with their own magic. Hiding its existence from
the world and more importantly, the queen.

Every summer, when the suns warmth shines at its
brightest, the ice melts and the water run's through
the mountain and into what is now known as the
River Vierg'e.

To capture the water is a treacherous quest. Doing so
comes at a hefty price. No mere mortal could ever
find it, though many have certainly tried.

The mystical Water Vierg'e fetches a high price on the
black market. Only those with wealth and the means
to find it, can afford it.

It is said to give the person who consumes it, the
temporary power of both the Faerie princess and the
Djinn prince combined. This I reserve for only the
most special of my guests.

For everyone else, there's a cheap bottled Evian in
the fridge.

I returned to my desk holding the glass of Vierg'e. The
clear pale blue liquid shimmering in the light of my
office.

The shiny liquid cast tiny star patterns in the light.
Projecting them across the walls and the ceiling, as it
bobbed within the small glass.

As I handed the glass over, I saw a flicker of surprise
cross over the Fairies face.

It was gone just as quickly as it came, blink and you
would have missed it entirely
I turned and walked away, pretending I hadn't seen
anything.
Causing the Faerie embarrassment would only wound
his pride. I returned to sit calmly in my chair.
The ancient forest folk may be bound to their ancient
rules but *we,* however, have never been bound to
anything. Nor will we ever be.
"A toast." I replied, with a soft smile, as I lifted my
glass, pausing as I held the glass to my lips.
The Faerie, raised his, politely in return.
"A toast." he replied, with a smile. Before greedily
putting the pure water to his lips and drank every last
drop, before placing his glass down heavily onto my
desk once he was done. His movements where
clumsy drunk from the instant effects of the water.
"My apologies, I do not know what has come over
me." He stammered, suddenly unsure of himself.
I smiled politely placing my still full glass down.
"Do you know the other half of the story king
Asperion.?" I didn't wait for him to answer before I
pressed on.
"Any Faerie king who consumes the water, gives up
his power as king, only to possess that which the
princess held.
His eyes widened, "No, it can't be true. Queen
Aaleyah! But... how?" He stammered, his face turning
to fear.

Leaning back into my chair, there was both an air of superiority and confidence that surrounded me. I smiled, more to myself than for his benefit.

"It was a cold winter evening, in January of, 1693. After the Awakening took place, I was kept locked in solid darkness by the God's for what felt like an eternity.

Then as I began to feel my life force begin to fade, I was thrown into Earth by the gods. Wet, naked and cold I lay in the forest stripped bare of all my memories and void of any identity.

Not long passed, as I lay in the freezing cold, when a young woman came by. Finding my disheveled body lying naked on the forest floor, she took pity upon me and took me to her home, hidden deep in the woodland. The next few days she nursed me back to health, gave me clean clothing and fed me.

I had never known such selflessness, and still to this day, I have not encountered anything like it again. She showed me how her magic could help the plants and the trees grow stronger. Using herb's, she had grown to brew potions that could cure almost any ailment. Her greatest magic of all was that she could perform a spell that allowed her to shapeshift into any living creature. She used this magic to reach impossible places, to gather ingredients for her potions. Transforming into a bird to fly to a mountain peak to collect a flower. Or transform into a squirrel so as to climb the tallest tree to collect honey.

On the third evening, just as we had sat down for a meal, a soft glow emerged from within the woods. Then, on the edge of our clearing we saw them. They came with flaming torches and bundles of wood. The young witch looked on in horror as the army of villagers circled the house and took us captive. They strung us both up to a tree and set wood at our feet. Then stood back to watch as they set us alight. The witch screamed as the flames licked hungrily at her body. Then as I stared into the fire burning at my feet, I felt something awaken inside of me. My memories came flooding back in a wave of power. I felt a hand wrap around my own as the young witch clasped onto me. In her final moments she uttered words I could not understand, but the magic that transferred into me was a language that I did understand. That was a feeling I knew well and one that I welcomed back with open arms. As the transfer of power finished, the young woman's body was burnt to ash in the flames. My body however, remained intact. For what is a Djinn queen of fire if she can burn to ashes. No, my magic protected me and my human shell. I looked out at the villagers as they looked at me in fear. I used my newfound ability to transform into the only other form I knew, my true form. I escaped those bonds and ravaged their village, until there was nothing left but ash."

I met his eyes. Those pale green eyes that, had once held so much wisdom and strength. Now looked paler, less confident...weak.

I looked deep into his soul through those green eyes.
Then I unleashed my smokeless fire, I willed my magic
to consume every corner of his being.

I reached deep within him and felt a rush of energy.
All his ancient magic and wisdom flowed through me
and I hungrily devoured it all.

I smelled the sweet smell of the forest, the muskiness
of the rich moss that grows in the undergrowth of the
great ancient trees. I felt the weight of forest realm
watching. As I glided through the ancient, green
woodland. I heard them whisper warnings to each
other through the wind and heard those warnings
glide with us through the forest air.

There was no hiding my existence from the world
now. Soon, all the creatures and beings would hear of
my presence. I did not care, for by the time the world
knew that the Djinn had returned and that I, had
possessed their precious king. It would be too late to
stop us.

All that mattered now, was to find the answer to my
one question. Where, is the location of the lost
Gue'dle amulet?

Chapter Eleven

On and on I flew past the ancient trees and through lush green ferns. I tasted the sweet dew as it dripped down, onto my skin.

The taste of honeysuckle was leaving a sticky sweet coating on the pillows of my lips.

Every sensation that I felt was exaggerated. It was almost too much for my subconscious to comprehend.

I could feel his heart begin to race, as the adrenaline coursed through his now tense body. I pushed my subconscious into him further, willing him to settle. He did not. I was left with the only option I had left, of taking more control over him. He struggled against me, only briefly.

Managing to scream out in his mind to me. 'NO!' 'We didn't agree to this!'

I felt his body go rigid, before I took full control of him.

His own mind now trapped, locked away forever inside a box of my doing.

'Enough distractions I must push on, this body cannot withstand much more. I must claim back what is rightfully *mine.*'

With that thought I re-focused, pushing forward with renewed haste.

The sun was hanging low in the sky, as the trees cast long shadows across the forest floor. Dusk enveloped the forest. No longer was there the sound of wind rushing through the trees. Now the forest came alive with the almost deafening sound of crickets and cicadas. as I drew closer to the base of the mountain, darkness fell on the rain forest. The floor once a green sea of ferns, now lay in darkness.

The Faerie folk where so in tune with their world, and in this realm, they were also linked to each other. It was how their very essence, their magic and their being had stayed alive for millions of years, evolving and growing through their evolution. They were so powerful that they may even outlive this world. I had been wrong; they weren't a dying species hiding in their forests, slowly waiting for time to allow them to fade. They were a beacon of power and what I felt made me scared. I had deluded myself into thinking that we had no need to worry ourselves about such things, our kind where safe.

We the *Djinn* are forever, just as we have always been.

I would never get used to how alive the faerie plain made me feel. feeling everything through a host was so real, and solidified.

Experiencing the world more intensely made my skin

feel as though it was coming alive with the different sensations. My senses where in overdrive, my mind was madly trying to catch up with the complexity of it all. Everything was being thrust upon me like waves crashing down on top of me.

One curse of our never ending existence was that we, as our own entities could not feel.

The only way it was possible for the *Djinn* to experience such things, was by inhabiting a host. One who's power matched ours or else they would burn out far too quickly. We had learned long ago that inhabiting normal humans was a waste. They were a weaker species and yet they ran like a plague through the world. So, we took to breeding with them, to even out the odds. Giving us adequate vessels each time we crossed through the veil.

Suddenly there it was, I could hear the sound of water trickling through a narrow stream. Then without warning, I was left standing in a large clearing. I looked up into the ancient trees that circled above.

They stood towering above the forest floor, stretching endlessly to the sky above. Their trunks where so large, that only a small space remained between each tree.

The ground felt soft and lush beneath my host's feet. I wriggled his toes with pleasure, the sensation sent a tickle through his body and a shiver up his spine. This vessel felt alive and full of wonder, this was the edge of the Faerie kingdom, clearly, he had not been so far away from home in a very long time.

I began to feel light and sleepy, as though all my troubles had been taken away.

"NO!"

I screamed wordlessly into the air, but no sound was audible in this place. Only the sound of the forest and the steady trickle of water from the River.

I shook myself, trying to remain focused. The Faerie magic sliding away like a thin veil of spider webs. He was fighting me trying to push me out I would not let him take over me. I pushed back, forcing my subconscious deeper into his mind, searching with force to unlock the secret that the Faerie King had been keeping hidden for thousands of years. I had a moment to feel success, then without warning the world went dark.

Slowly light filtered through the darkness. When the light grew strong enough, I could see that I was now standing in a new clearing.

King Asperion had used the last of his magic to cloud my mind just long enough to hide the secret passageway into the hidden cave. Now we were outside the kingdoms border, he had no power here, this was the temple of the Gods themselves.

Luckily being a Djinn I was capable of crossing realms leaving my powers intact. 'Well...for the moment anyway.' I pushed the thought aside and stared in wonder at my surroundings.

The cave was oval. large stalagmites, glittering with jewels hung down from the caves ceiling. Three trees grew around the center of the cave close together as if they could hold out their branches and link together in a circle.

Their remaining leaves where illuminated by a warm glow of sunlight that streaked through a circular opening, that had been formed centuries ago in the rock.

It was Autumn not spring here and the ground was hard. There was no green moss laying underfoot. Only hard cracked dirt and stone that lay covered by dry Autumn leaves, littered the cave floor.

Their vibrant colours emanated the feeling of warmth, in the cool crisp autumn air. An assortment of colours littered the cavern floor from the fallen leaves. Bright yellow's, brown's and orange's, lay in an autumn rainbow.

The sound of the river reverberated through the cave, the river itself flowed right through the mountain. I looked at the three trees as they stood growing in the sunlight. Their bark smooth and gleaming as white as bone.

I could see a shimmer in the air in front of the clustered trees. It was as though heat emanated up from the ground, from only that one space. I knew then that this was the place, this was where we needed to be.

'Finally, after all our years of searching, after risking

my own being becoming lost, or possibly destroyed by faerie magic. We were finally going to find the answer to the one question we so desperately sought.'

Chapter Twelve

I sat in the dimly lit hotel suite, resting as much as I could in the cream upholstered tub chair that sat at the side of the room. Sipping on the second whiskey that I'd greedily taken from the mini bar. I savoured the smell as its pungent aroma filled my senses with the promise of a burning warmth. Alcohol didn't affect me in the way that it affected others, but I could still enjoy it for the taste and warmth it brang in the bitter cold July weather.

The two double beds took up what was left of the cramped space. The brick walls of the room created an almost claustrophobic effect. An attempt had been made by the hotel management to disguise that with an oversized picture of the Australian outback. The twelve hundred centre metre wide painting hung haphazardly in the centre of the brick wall directly over the two beds. I resisted the urge to straighten it up, as I marvelled at the intricate detail the artist had put into painting the bark and sap of a eucalyptus tree.

Danny came in from the bathroom, then sat on the edge of the bed looking worried. He stared at me for a heartbeat before speaking.

"We have to tell her the whole truth, she will never agree to go with us otherwise."

I shook my head. "No. She's not ready, I will decide when the time is right." I said firmly.

"But..." I held up my hand to silence his argument.

Sighing deeply, I took the last swig from my glass. The ice cubes clinking against each other. As I placed the glass down on the small bedside table that was between us. Danny stood abruptly, clearly annoyed. He threw his arms in the air as he turned and walked to the other bed, where his laptop lay charging.

"Still stubborn after all these years. You are so much like her sometimes, do you know that?"

I took in a deep breath. I was tired, we had been travelling for a year, barely stopping more than a few days in one place. We had been to most of Europe, the Middle East, America and now Australia.

Of all the times I had dreamed of coming to Australia, not once did I imagine that it would be under these circumstances.

Sophia burst into the room, a look of fear and anger was on her face. She turned towards Danny and then back to me.

"Both of you had better start talking because I am not leaving anywhere with you, until I get some well deserved answers."

her finger was pointing wildly from one to the both of us as she spoke with force.

She was clearly angry, and I knew that she didn't even know the half of what she was angry about.

I felt an overwhelming feeling of sadness and sympathy right then. Sophia had spent her life living a lie and where it not for the events of this past year, she would have continued to live a blissfully ignorant normal life.

Instead both Sophia and Juliana would now be thrown out to sea without a life raft and left with no way of ever coming back. their lives would now be altered forever.

I had the answers but not the ones Sophia needed. I could see she wanted to be told it was all a cruel joke, that we would leave and that she would never have to see either of us again. Secretly I knew she didn't truly believe that, deep down inside her she knew she was different. That she had always been different to everyone else. Soon she would know the truth, that

the visions where only a tiny part of her true potential.

Sophia was still yelling, and it took everything I had to pull myself from my own thoughts and back to the moment at hand.

"Did you hear me!" Sophia screeched at me.

"I asked why the fuck you need me? How do you both 'seem' to know both Jules and I so well?" The last she said with extreme sarcasm even making quotation marks in the air. All I could do to not aggravate her even more was sit there nod silently at her.

"Ok." I finally replied after pausing to gather my thoughts.

"Your right, you deserve answers. All of them, so please sit and let me explain."

"Can I get you a drink Sophia?" Danny chimed in trying to smooth the situation over.

"Yes, a vodka and lemonade." She replied snappily, while rubbing at her temples.

"I can't reach Jules on her phone, I've tried multiple times, but it just goes through to voice mail."

Danny opened the mini fridge and grabbed out a can of lemonade and a cold glass.

"I'll have another whiskey." I said.

Nodding, Danny grabbed my glass and went back over to the tiny kitchenette counter. I turned to Sophia and smiled a soft smile.

"Firstly, I am sorry, all of this is so much to take in. However, after I explain everything to you, I hope that you will understand my need for urgency."

"Long ago before humans and animals, back when the Earth was only new. There existed two realms. The first realm was home to what we know now as Earth. This was home to the forest folk or as you know them, *Faerie's*. The other realm was made entirely of darkness. So empty was this realm, that nothing had feeling or even substance. It is known as the..." Sophia held up her hand.

"I know its name, it's the in between. I'm sure I've been there, or at least it felt real in my dream."
Sophia paused looking expectantly at me for an answer. I sat back in my chair and pressed on.
"Yes, it is called the in between. It is where the Djinn have lived for their entire existence. Just like the Faerie folk, they are immortal.
That is why they have no body and just like the image you saw in that video. Appear as a cloud of smoke.
The Djinn grew tired of living in the darkness and they wanted to grow in the Faerie kingdom and take over the earth. The Faerie King knew that the only way for the Djinn to live here was by possessing a host and even then, they could not sustain that for eternity. One day the prince of the Djinn crossed over the in between to the forest folk and spoke to King Asperion.
His plan was to marry the princess whom he loved as she was his perfect opposite, together they would create a perfect balance of light and dark. He knew that their love was forbidden but, he also knew that the secret to the Djinn and the Faerie's alliance rested on the two of them being bound together for eternity.
Almost like a contract but with souls instead of a signed contract. The prince also knew that if they produced an heir that the child would be of mixed blood. A perfect combination of the two, resulting in the Djinn being able to live in the Faeries realm

peacefully."

Sophia lent forward completely engaged.

"So, what happened?" She asked.

"Well, what always happens with a forbidden love. The Djinn Queen Aaleyah found out and thinking only of her own greed and lust for power, she kidnapped the princess. Her plan was to take over the Faerie kingdom for her own. If she could release the djinn into the realm, they could possess every fey and wipe them out once and for all. Of course, the prince fought back. There is nothing more dangerous than a man in love. He vowed to find the princess and bring about the exile of the Djinn as punishment so he could live with the princess in peace."

I paused to take a sip of my drink before continuing.

"He knew his power was no match for the Queen alone. So, he did the only thing he could. He asked the Faerie king for help. The king in his grief blindly agreed and gave the prince the power to get the princess back."

"What did he do?" Asked Sophia eagerly.

"He gave him his eldest son to possess. And by doing so he knew that there was no return for either of them. Because you must understand Sophia, that once a Djinn possesses the host. It cannot be undone, especially when the power is equal to that of the Djinn itself."

"Wow, so a prince for a prince, that's pretty morbid." Sophia looked appalled at the idea.

"When the prince bonded with the Faerie princes' body, he allowed them both to have equal consciousness. It's what's called the grand conjoining. Together in the one body they hatched a plan to rescue the princess and to close the doorway to the in between forever."

"unfortunately, it was not to be. The prince found the princess hidden in the tallest peak of the highest mountain locked inside a crystal prison.

Overwhelmed by despair as both prince's hearts where breaking simultaneously. They lay at the foot of the princess' prison and admitted defeat. Hearing the mourning prayers of the two princes, the gods responded to their pleas. The tears of the God's rained upon the mountain and this created what is known as the mystical water *Vierg'e.* And in turn protecting them from the queen ever finding them. In the hopes that one day someone with power as strong as the gods themselves can find the hidden location and free them all.

"But hang on, I thought they were immortal. If that's so then how are any of them dead?"

"Ah' but I never said they were dead, only entombed."

"Oh, so what happened next, did the king Aspera... whatever his name is go searching for them all or what?"

I chuckled. "King Asperion. And no one knows. All I know for sure is that the precious water Vierg'e has been written about for centuries. You know of it; it's also been called the fountain of youth."

Chapter Thirteen

I couldn't help myself, I just started laughing. "Ok Dr Amiri, you got me, that was a great story, now if you'll both excuse me I'm going to jump in the first cab back to straight - Ville and leave you two crazies here in loony town."

I stood up. "I can't believe that they even thought for a second I would buy that load of crap."

I looked over at Dr Amiri he had a stern look on his face.

"Come on you can't be serious. You. An archaeological expert actually believes that story!"

"Sophia, after everything you have seen today do you really think there isn't even the tiniest possibility that all of this could be real?"

I paused.

"No. That video has to be fake. I mean anyone can create that on their laptop, special effect programs are as easy to buy as a packet of chips these days."

"There's more you need to know, please sit back down." Once again, I was being asked to sit.

"Fine." I said grumpily and sat down on the bed. My arms crossed tightly over my chest.

"Many great rulers searched for the fountain of youth, but no one ever revealed to have found it, but Danny and I suspect that one great ruler did find it."
"Who?" I said my eyes narrowing in suspicion.
"Queen Cleopatra mysteriously vanished in what appears to be the greatest love story of all time. Danny show her what we found." he said pointing to the laptop.
Danny walked over to his laptop and picked it up, before sitting beside me he scrolled through a series of photos from their archaeological site.
There on the next photo stood a small glass vial, the lid was made from what appeared to be gold.
It had a slight discolouration covering it from aging. The vial was resting on what looked to be a ledge of sorts made of red granite. The contents where half gone, and the remains had stuck like glue to the side of the glass.
The screen flicked to another photo.
Danny was holding the vial up to the sunlight and the dried contents inside gleamed like tiny stars.
"This vial was found two years ago. We ran lab tests to try to determine what the contents where. We found things in that vial that don't even exist on earth naturally. Only ever seen in tests conducted on meteorites!"
"So, let me get this straight. You found a "magic" vial of meteorite stuff and you think it's this water Vierg'e?"

Danny shoved the laptop over to me and I was staring
at a painted wall full of hieroglyphic's and pictures
depicting a queen drinking a blue liquid and going
into battle, with what appeared to be a dark wisp of
smoke at her back.
"Ok so even if this was all true, what does this have
to do with Jules and I being in danger?"
"We think that Queen Cleopatra not only found the
river but that she harnessed its power. We believe
that Cleopatra in her delve into alchemy and the
magic's. That she may have made a deal with the
devil, so to speak. i.e.; Queen Aaleyah."
"Hold on Danny, that doesn't make any sense. If she
made the deal, then why is this Djinn going around
on a killing spree now?"
Dr Amiri cleared his throat.
"If I may, you see Cleopatra made the amulet. She
found a way to split the Djinn and the Faeries powers
into separate elements. Unfortunately, she
disappeared, and no one knows what happened to
her, or the amulet and yet it's here, in almost every
painting we have seen."
"So, you guy's think that the Queen is sending out
one of her Djinn to look for the amulet?"
"YES!" They both exclaimed together. "Ok, so what
happens if he finds it?"
Dr Amiri and Danny exchanged a look. "Well are one
of you going to tell me or are you just going to stare
at each other all afternoon?"

Danny sat back down on the edge of the bed. They both looked completely worn out. There was a tightness around his eyes that I hadn't noticed before.

Danny turned to me, a pleading look on his face, accompanied by a deep sorrow in his eyes. "It's not a he, it's a she."

"Okay..." I said waiting for Danny to continue. It's complicated and hard to explain. But one thing is for certain if the queen finds out that you have powerful visions, she will hunt you down and try to use you."

Silence filled the room. Finally, Danny spoke breaking the silence.

"We need your visions to help us locate the entrance to the hidden chamber."

"What! That's not even possible. I only have visions in my dreams. And most of them feel more like memories." I said sounding baffled.

"That's exactly why we need you Sophia, you have been given a gift. One that could bring about the greatest archaeological find since king Tutankhamen was discovered." Danny looked at me pleadingly.

"Sophia, we need you to come with us, we think we may know where the amulet is hidden."

Dr Amiri sounded impatient now.

"Ok. Ok. So, we've established that you both have a theory. But what happens if we run into the Djinn Queen on the way?" I asked looking at both of them.

"That is why time is so important, we must leave

tonight if we are to reach the cave before she finds out about your powers and follows our steps."

I nodded in agreement. 'I can't believe I'm about to do this.' I thought. I'm so out of my own mind right now.

With that thought I left the loonies to their plans and their frantic packing and went back outside to the car to think about what an insane decision I'd just made.

Chapter Fourteen

The door closed as Sophia exited the room. I secretly hoped that she wouldn't try to run. Her own life was hanging entirely in the wind. The longer she stayed here, the less chance she had of staying alive.

"She needs more time, to come into her true powers." I turned to Dr Amari as he spoke.

"You didn't tell her the truth, you only told her part of the truth, you need to tell her the full truth about who she really is before it's too late." Dr Amiri looked calmly at me.

I didn't calm down I was angry, so I just yelled.

"And what of Jules, what do we tell her?" He sighed before replying.

"Nothing, she will find out on her own very soon."

"And when she does, what will you do then?" I spat my words at him.

"We will protect her." He flatly replied.

"Sometimes, I think you truly only care about what's in your own selfish best interest *prince* Amiri." I spat, letting the distain show in my voice.

"I am in no mood for your sarcasm, the same could be said for you Prince Leos, need I remind you that it's your crazy mother who's out there killing both of our people."

I sighed, admitting defeat. "I am not like her, you know that."

"I know, I've been inside your head remember." replied Amiri as he gently laid a hand on my shoulder. "We must stay focused on our task. We cannot afford to get distracted. Too many lives have been lost already."

I nodded in stern agreement.

"Many more will be lost if she finds out we are free from that tomb Amiri."

"All the more reason why, we must leave for the airport now. I will call and organise the jet."

"I wish we could use our powers; I feel so vulnerable." I sounded childish even after all these years. You would think I would have grown a backbone by now but no, not when it came to my mother and her vicious temper.

"You know we can't, Danus. She will sense us straight away. My greatest fear is already coming true. The longer we linger here, the stronger Sophia becomes in our presence. The power is searching for her and Juliana, trying to find its way back to them."

With that he grabbed his mobile phone and walked outside after Sophia into the cool afternoon air.

~ PARABELLUM ~

Chapter Fifteen

Jones cracked his neck as we pulled up to the crime scene. A habit of his that had always made me cringe at the sound. The house stood dark and deserted, even the street lay quiet in the heavy afternoon glow. After the busy morning it had received just hours before, it felt almost alien to be out in the deserted street. Even if we were sitting hidden inside our car. I looked at the time, it was 2:45pm. Winter always made the day's feel darker. As though the shortened days teamed with the constant coldness, always made the days feel suspended, in that short time between evening and dusk. When the light slowly fades until true dark hits the sky in a sea of black. Winter was always hard in our small town, but this year had felt colder.

Another murder had rocked our nation. The tenth one in six months. All of them where exactly the same. Nothing in the house is ever disturbed except for the victims. Who are left tortured, mutilated and their empty carcasses then left lying dead in their bed's. There was something disturbing about that, all on its own. Your home is your safe haven.

Your bed is the place you curl up into when you are at your most vulnerable. Whether that be from exhaustion at the end of a long day, or when you're sick and can't move. The thought sent a shiver down my spine. Then there where the other parts of the case that made us all feel scared.

There were no fingerprints, no DNA and no signs of a struggle. There was also no evidence of forced entry to the house at all.

Every door was locked from the inside and was still locked when the police arrived. We had to force our way through the front door and what we found was the same as the other ten crime scenes.

One house had so many locks and protective screens, that the police had to break in through the roof. When they reached the manhole, they found it was bolted shut.

So, they had to bust a hole in the ceiling to get inside. The killer's motive is always the same.

The victim is asleep in their bed, then they are completely stripped of all their internal organs. The skin is removed, from the head down and the waist up.

There are no knife marks on the bodies whatsoever. Miraculously not one of the victims seem to have woken up. Yet their eyes are staring blankly upwards. The doctors and specialists are completely baffled. They have no brain trauma consistent with the trauma they went through, it's as though they just fell asleep and never woke up.

During our search of the house, we found books and paraphernalia of a group called, the Philosophical society. Ongoing research in this case revealed hundreds more unsolved murders, scattered out all over the world dating back hundreds of years.

Every single one matching our crime scene. All the victims appear to be linked with the same organization.

Jones believes it's a family of serial killers we are hunting. Masked as a hate crime. As an added bonus they take the internal organs. Presumably to sell on the black market. leaving the victims displayed as if to send a message. I think it's a great theory, it certainly does fit the profile we are seeing in the evidence trail. *And* we have absolutely zilch else to go on. We have worked our asses off on this case for the last six months and have found absolutely nothing.

No leads, no witnesses, absolutely zero physical evidence...Until today.

Forensics had found traces of an unknown substance, at one of the previous crime scenes. It had been embedded into the carpet beside the victim's bed. For the first time ever, our murderer had slipped up. Our specialists had spent dyes trying to run this through the system, called every scientist we could. Then the lab guys finally came back with a positive match.

It was molten. When we found out we thought there

must have been a mistake, but there wasn't. Now for the million dollar question. Where the hell had it come from? We were thousands of kilometers Away from an active volcano! And it's not like molten just happens to get randomly stuck to your shoe in transit like chewing gum. That stuff would melt the damn shoe. And would leave behind a stump for a leg.

I pictured the pain that molten would cause our perp. I sat for a moment, lost in the joyous thought of the murderer getting what he deserved. Pain being inflicted onto him for a change. Made to feel helpless, like he was nothing more than a piece of meat. Just like he did to all of his victims.

The lab is trying to retrieve the video recordings on the security cameras. The lab was sending it over for Jones and I to view. I'm holding my breath we may finally have some hard evidence, that we can use to point us into the right direction.

Thirty minutes ago, one of the neighbors called in. Claiming that they could see movement inside the house. They thought that there was someone poking around inside.

So here we are, primed and ready for action. Both of us secretly hoping that we can start to get some answers. We were getting desperate, we had everyone breathing down our necks wanting answers. Unfortunately for a cop, that's pretty dangerous territory to be walking in. The last thing we need is for the media to start sensationalizing things and making the public go into panic mode.

I turned to Jones, "Ready?"

He gave a curt nod.

"Good. Then let's do this."

We both got out of the car, closing over our doors gently so we didn't make a lot of noise.

The fence had been opened. The padlock was cut and discarded on the ground. Pulling out or guns we snuck through the fence before we hurried towards the front door.

Reaching the front step as quietly as possible. The front door was ajar and the police tape that sealed the door had been cut and partially removed.

We paused, and Jones signaled silently to me that we would go on three.

Being cautious we stood firmly on either side of the front door. He mouthed silently too me *One. Two...*

On three Jones pushed open the door, walking through briskly, his shoulders squared and tense.

I held my gun, pointing it out in front of my face, at eye level. I was tense, but careful to remain flexible in case I had to jerk back at the last minute.

We were in the entry hall scanning all sides. In the center of the hall was a flight of stairs that led to the upstairs bedrooms. On the left of me, held what appeared to be the dining room.

On the other side of Jones was the lounge room. We swapped sides, he went left, I went right.

As I entered the lounge room, I stood straight, with

my back to the wall scanning the room. It was clear. I quickly scanned the room, nothing appeared to have been disturbed.

The sound of my heart was thumping in my ears. I took a few deep breaths to calm my nerves. I felt my heartbeat begin to slow. I turned and went to join Jones in the dining room.

Just as I went to walk out of the room, I was deafened by the sound of gun shots ringing through the house. Followed by a deep groan followed by a hard thump. With my gun aimed I scanned the entry hall while hiding behind the wall listening.

I heard soft footsteps and the sound of a floorboard creaking.

I held my breath. My heart had worked its way up into my throat. I knew Jones was down otherwise he would have called out to me. I was lucky to be standing on carpet, floorboard free. As cautiously as I could, I stepped through the room. Making my way towards the back of the house. To where the kitchen and laundry where located.

My gun was pointed, I was ready for anything.

I heard another creak; I knew the assailant was close. I took a deep breath, steadying myself. My pulse was jumping in my throat.

I reached the doorway and crept silently towards the left side of the door frame. I stood half a meter back beside the door, my right shoulder pressed to the wall. My gun was aimed at the doorway.

If the intruder walked through, I had a clear shot, that would hit him before he knew I was there. I waited silently; my heart eased back into its normal rhythm. I stood there mustering all the patience in the world. Another creak of the floorboards and this time it was closer. I saw the silhouette of my target before the intruder carelessly walked right into my trap. I pulled the trigger hitting the assailant in their right arm.

A scream quickly followed as he fell to the floor. The gun in his hand falling carelessly onto the carpet. Quickly without wasting any time I moved towards the assailant, I kicked the gun out of the way so it couldn't be used again.

Without wasting any time, I knelt down and restrained my now crying gunman, with a pair of hand cuffs. Which I pulled out from the pouch on my police belt.

Another scream bellowed out of him, as I twisted his arm behind his back, cuffing him. After ensuring he was properly restrained, I flipped him over onto his back only to find with surprise that in fact 'he' was really a she.

I pulled my portable radio off of my belt and turned the volume back on and radioed in for back up and an ambulance. "officer down!" I screeched into the radio. My voice sounding high pitched and frantic.

I pulled the mystery girl to her feet.

Pushing her into the dining room so that I could keep an eye on her while I checked out Jones. I was too busy watching my prisoner and not where I was going. Tripping I landed face first on the cold floorboards. I heard my prisoner go down too with a thump followed by a scream of agony.

I could feel blood pouring from my lip which had obviously split on impact. Dazed I looked around the dimly lit room. To my horror I saw Jones. My heart sank down to my stomach, I had tripped over his seemingly lifeless body that lay sprawled out on the dining room floor. Just a meter from the doorway. A thick mass of dark blood pooled around him.

Suddenly I saw movement from the corner of my eye. My female prisoner let out a high pitched, terrified scream. As she stumbled backwards into the corner of the room.

I turned towards the movement, holding my gun out in front of me. A dark figure appeared.

I got off two shots, before the thing de-materialized. Before I could react, it came at me. Engulfing me in what was now just a cloud of black smoke.

The force of it pushed my body back, with unimaginable strength. I smashed my head into the hard floor. I felt as though I was falling, as if the ground turned to liquid beneath my body.

Everything went dark as I began to lose consciousness. I could hear a voice call to me from the shadows. I couldn't move. My body was pinned down. I felt cold and alone, trapped in the growing darkness.

Chapter Sixteen

I was floating, with no feeling of emotion or physical pain. It felt as though I was just in a black pool of existence. I couldn't hold onto a thought long enough to give it feeling. A voice whispered through me, with an accent that I couldn't recognise. The voice was heavy and held power. As though it could reach intimate parts of my soul. That I never knew existed, until this very moment.

"Juliana don't be afraid. I will not hurt you my child."

"Who are you? Why are you doing this?"

"I knew you would find me eventually, and you are so close. But I cannot have that. Not when I am so near to achieving my, true goal."

"Where am I?"

"I have you in my kingdom. It is known only as, the In between. It is the home of the Djinn, your true home. I bought you here to show you, who you really are."

Pictures flashed through my mind, of dark figures made of shadow. Each shadow had its own unique colour. The voice spoke again, this time clearer. "We are the almighty Djinn, we have always been, just as we will always be. We have been around since the dawn of time. We were happy once; our kingdom wasn't always this desolate place. Once upon a time, long ago we were a part of your world. Worshipped as gods, we walked among you. We were free and happy. We kept the balance of Earth in perfect harmony, working alongside the Faeries, our magic helped Earth to grow and thrive. But alas, it was not to last. A great struggle for power erupted between the Djinn and the fey. They trapped us in what is known as the second realm, her in the In between. We need you to help us Juliana, for you are the key. I have searched for you for hundreds of years." I almost had you were it not for those bumbling inbred bogans. What's that saying, you humans say. Ah' yes. 'If you want something done right, you have to do it yourself!' That was my mistake."

But I knew that I could get your attention, that was the easy part. The hard part was that I needed to get you alone. To show you the truth that has been kept from you for so long.

"You killed my parents! Why? what did they ever do to you!"

"They were not your real parents Juliana. They were only your adoptive parents. You know that. Your identity has been hidden from you. They knew, and they lied to you for years."

Anger flared inside me like I had never felt before. Something inside me stirred, something dark that I had never felt before. Hot piercing warmth rose through my chest before I pushed it forcefully out of me. I lashed out in the dark. tearing at it as though I had claws. I imagined each layer tearing away, revealing light behind its seemingly black walls. The darkness withdrew, as if hurt. Slowly, the air became easier to breath as I gulped in huge lungsful of air. I could feel the cold floor beneath me. As the light stung at my eyes.

I lay on my back, waiting for the world to stop spinning. When I felt like I wasn't going to pass out again, I slowly sat up.

My mystery woman was out cold. Blood stained her shirt where the bullet had hit her shoulder. The sound of sirens echoed outside. I crawled on all fours, over to Jones who lay in a heap beside me. I felt for a pulse. There was none. I immediately began CPR. Police came bursting through the door. "Clear!" They yelled as they secured the rest of the house. "Jesus Christ! Get the fucking ambo's in here would ya! Officer Jones is down!" Yelled one of the policemen. I ignored the hustle of officers scrambling behind me. As I put everything I had into pumping on Jones' chest. The ambulance officers burst in, pulling me away. All I could do was watch in horror as they put the defibrillator paddles to his chest and tried to jump start his heart. I looked down at my hands which were now shaking. Stained crimson with Jones' blood.

The Ambo's stopped trying to resuscitate Jones and

called it. *"Death at 13:00 hours on July 4th, 2020."* My
heart began to race, my head started to spin, as tiny
prickles of shock coursed through my entire body. I
couldn't breathe. I pushed my way outside before
hurling yet again, into the rose bushes.

I sat back on the grass, my head resting on my raised
knee. my phone began to ring in my pocket. I pulled it
out, checking the caller I.D. Just as the gurney was
being wheeled inside by the ambulance officers. It
was Sophie. I answered the call, my hand shaking as I
raised the phone to my ear. My hands now sticky with
Jones' dried blood.

"Jules, are you there? Hello!" Sophia's urgent voice
rang in my ear, forcing me to move the receiver
further away.

"Yeah, I'm here." I replied. My voice sounded cracked
and hoarse.

"Jules, you have to meet me. It's about your case!
You're in danger!" She bellowed down the phone, her
voice becoming impatient.

"I know." I replied flatly. There was a pause.

"What? But...how?"

I'll explain later, Jones is dead. Look I've got to go."
I said and hung up on her. My voice sounded distant
and detached. Shock was good like that.

A police officer came out with constable Smith
trailing closely behind.

"Jules, are you ok?" Smith asked giving me a
concerned look.

"Do I look like I'm fucking ok?"
"No, I'm sorry...That. That was a stupid question." he
stammered.
Then he turned, his hand balling into a fist.
"Fuck, I'm so sorry Jules. You tried everything you
could."
I glared at Smith; no words could describe the anger I
was feeling in that moment. Then something inside
me let go, and a flood of tears quickly replaced the
anger. I sat on the grass curled in a ball, squeezing my
legs tightly against my body, and I cried.

The ride back to the station, felt like an eternity. The
ambulance officers had checked me over after they
had taken Jones' body. As soon as they were done,
we left the other constables behind to secure the
crime scene. Then we made our way back to the
station.
Smith turned from the front passenger seat to give
me words of comfort. I wasn't listening. I sat in the
back seat, staring blankly out the window as we
pulled into the south side police station, car park at
the side of the building.
The Large metal security gate slid open and we pulled
into our designated car space.
Smith jumped out, opening the door for me. You
can't open a rear police door from the inside, its child

locked to keep the bad guys, who are usually locked in there from jumping out. Usually given half a chance, at the first set of traffic lights you pull up to. We made our way into the police station via the rear security entrance of the building. We were greeted by constable Grey, as we entered the office hallway.

"Jules, I'm sorry. Sargent Davis wants to see you in his office, right away."

I nodded, still not able to speak.

Smith walked with me down the hallway, to Sargent Davis' office. He knocked once, before a deep voice said 'come in.'

when we got inside, Sargent Davis was behind his desk, typing up a report on his computer.

He was a big man, he was broad shouldered and tall just like Jones, but larger in the middle.

His hair was flecked with grey and white streaks. But I had to admit, at fifty years old, he was doing pretty well. I knew people I went to school with who, went full grey by the age of thirty.

Sargent Davis stopped typing and turned to face us.

"Jules, first and foremost I'm sorry that this has happened."

"Thank you." I managed to say softly.

Davis gave a deep breath out before continuing.

"Jules, you have personal leave available. I want you to take it. I think you need some time to process. And I want you to get some grief counselling immediately."

Anger welled up inside me. "But Sarge, the case! The killer is still out there..." He held up a hand silencing me. "I know and Constable Smith will be taking over the investigation. You are no good to this investigation at the moment. I have a responsibility for your health and wellbeing, so please. Do as I have asked. Go and write your report, Constable Smith will take your statement. One of the other constables can drive you home."

I took in a deep breath; I knew it was pointless arguing. "Sure." is all I said. leaving it at that.

As I walked out of the office, and into the interview room. I felt defeated, everything had been taken out of my hands now. I had no way of finding the killer. Then, a thought occurred to me. Remembering the phone call. How did Sophie know? what was she babbling about before I cut her off? I turned quickly back down the hallway. Straight back into Sargent Davis' office. "Sarge, can I please do this interview in the morning. My head is really aching from my fall, I think I need to go straight home." "Yes, of course." He replied, suddenly looking more concerned. He picked up his office phone and asked one of the constables to come in. A young constable named William came in. "I need you to take a quick walk with Jules, make sure she gets home to her apartment ok. Its only five minutes away." "Sure, I'll just go let Sharon know." With that he turned and left, coming back a minute later. "Ok, you all ready?" he asked.

"Yep, let's go." I said. And off we went. Five minutes later I was in my lounge room saying thank you to William as he walked out the apartment door. As soon as the door closed, I grabbed my phone. Pulling up my recent call list. I quickly pressed on Sophie's name and waited impatiently for her to pick up.

Chapter Seventeen

My phone buzzed loudly in my pocket. The vibration
sent a wave through my thigh. I yanked my phone
out. 'Thank God it was Jules.' I let out a deep sigh
before I answered.

"What the hell Jules, I've been waiting for the past
hour and a half for you to call me back. What the hell
happened?" I was pissed and felt scared.

"Look it's a long story, where are you?" Jules sounded
tired. I tried to remain calmer as I replied.

"I'm at the hotel near the airport. Can you get here
it's urgent? There's things we need to discuss."

"I'll get an Uber. I can't drive I've smashed my head.
I'll be there as soon as I can."

We hung up Jules sounded worn out.

I felt edgy, something was wrong I could feel it. It
wasn't just hearing that Jules had hurt her head. Or
the news that Jones was dead. No. It was more than
that.

I had been feeling uneasy since 3pm. It was as if a
light bulb had come on in my mind. Suddenly without
warning I collapsed on the concrete step outside the
hotel room. I was once again swimming in darkness

except this time it was Jules I was seeing. She was trapped in the In between, with the Queen. My visions had never been during the day, let alone about Jules.

That had never happened before. I should have felt scared, but I didn't. As the scene played out before me, I saw Jules reach out with her hand, Long claws appeared where her nails should have been. She grabbed at the darkness, tearing as she went. Slowly strip by strip was pulled back to reveal the light of day once more. I could see her partner Jones, lying in a pool of his own blood beside her. I saw Jules try to resuscitate him. I saw the ambulance crew coming in and pulling her away. I saw Jules run outside and throw up. And I saw her answer her phone. As I came to, Danny and Amiri where on either side of me. I was now lying on the bed.

"You collapsed on the front step, so we bought you inside." Danny whispered.

I sat up the room swam. I pressed my hands over my eyes as I spoke. "Jules. She's on her way here now. We need to protect her!" I said and I was scared. Danny and Amiri looked puzzled.

"I didn't faint, I just had a vision. And a bloody good one at that!" I then told them what I had seen, and about Jules' claws ripping the in between to shreds. Jules was safe I knew that. I just needed her to get here, time was running out. I knew that now.

I pulled my phone out. "I need to call her again; see

how far away she is."
The phone was ringing. On the third ring she
answered.
"Jules how far away are you?"

"I've just pulled into the car park of the hotel."
"Ok I'm coming out now."
I ignored the thumping migraine in my head as I
dashed out the door, just as Jules was exiting the
Uber. She saw me and a look of relief came over her
face.
"Oh' Sophia. God am I glad to see you!" She hugged
me. Holding me close to her so tightly, that I thought I
was going to pass out again.
"Quick come inside, we need to talk."
It took about thirty minutes for all four of us to
exchange stories. It helped that I had, had a vision of
what had happened. That cut out the awkwardness
of Jules having to find a way to try and tell me, that
she grew claws in another realm. Without sounding
like a complete fruit cake.
We told Jules the history of the Queen and about the
ancient Gue'dle Amulet.
The only question that Jules had at the end of it all
was why the queen thought that Jules was the key.
Good question I thought considering that I thought
she was tracking both of us.
Dr Amiri stood against the mini bar, a look of deep
concern and thoughtfulness creased his brow.

"I think that its plausible to assume. That the Queen doesn't know that you exist Sophie."

"We can use this to our advantage." Danny chimed in. Dr Amiri nodded in response.

"We need to leave; the plane is ready for us. If we leave now, we can make it to the base of the mountain by night fall."

With that we grabbed our belongings and got hurriedly into the car.

The private airfield was behind the main airport, it took five minutes of fighting through the afternoon traffic to get out of the domestic terminal car park. Before we were on the main road that led to the private hangar. When we arrived we were greeted by the security guard. Who after checking Dr Amiri's I.D let us through.

The jet was a small white jet with blue stripes running along its side. Danny stood beside me. "Impressive huh'. It's a Lear jet 45XR, one of the fastest business jets in the world. Also, one of the few that can carry a heavy load and not have its speed compromised."

Danny smiled like a school kid that was given the brownie point award for being the smartest kid in the classroom. I gave him a weak smile, in recognition. I had the urge to pat him on his head and say good boy. I resisted the urge.

Dr Amiri stood on the top step and ushered for us to hurry up and get in.

Once inside I had a moment of being in utter awe. To

say that the interior of the jet was impressive was an understatement.

I sat beside Jules, resting comfortably into one of the plush pale leather seats of the jet.

Dr Amiri sat across from us, resting his loosely clasped hands together on the polished wooden table. That extended from the side of the plane under the window, outwards, creating a barrier between us. Danny sat on the long couch, on the other side of the plane. Turning slightly so he was gazing patiently out of the small window. We sat patiently as we waited for the captain to start the engines.

Looking around, I marveled at how elaborate the interior of the small jet was. There was the same polished wood framed all around the bar area, which was at the back of the plane on the right hand side. Beside it was a short hallway which led to the bathroom.

There was a set of half moon couches. Set along the opposite walls behind us that took up the rear area of the plane. Both held two small round wooden coffee tables, to place your drinks on.

The plane had not one, but two large flat screen televisions. Which you could view from every seat in the jet.

"Who owns this jet, Beyoncé and Jay Z?" I said with a giggle. "On a serious note though. How can you afford all of this?"

Dr Amiri gave a small smile. "Let's just say that, I have

a lot of wealthy parties who are very generous with their investments."

"Hmm, how very diplomatic of you. Yes, thanks for clearing that up." I said letting the heavy sarcasm drip strongly in my voice.

"Your lapel, it is extremely elegant. I have never seen a broch like it."

Smiling gently Dr Amiri ran his index finger across the smooth blue stone.

"Yes, I suppose it is quite rare, it was a gift." He replied.

I lent closer over the table to get a better look. From this close I could now see the gold that surrounded the gemstone. It was in fact a serpent, wrapped tightly around in a circle clutching the gem. Its tail was inside its open mouth as though it was eating itself.

I gasped. "It can't be!" Jules exclaimed in surprise. Danny turned at her sudden outburst.

Looking down at his hand, as it subconsciously slid across his knee as he turned back from the window. I was staring into a large emerald ring, with the same serpent encircling it.

She turned furious eyes to both of them.

"Who are you really? I mean one minute no one has ever heard of you, then all of a sudden you make a huge discovery."

She said wildly gesturing at Dr Amiri.

"And yet you both have the same insignia on your

jewellery!" I knew the serpent well. I had studied the Theosophical society when I was in my first year of uni. They had been criticized continually over the years. "Are you a part of the Theosophical society Dr Amiri?" I asked, my head cocked slightly to the side, studying his reaction.

Dr Amiri let out a boisterous laugh that echoed through the entire cabin. I could see Jules furrow her brow in disapproval.

"No." he finally managed to say, shaking his head. "We are not."

Jules lent forwards; her anger came off her like a volatile cobra about to strike.

"It's very convenient, that you two show up at the same time that we find out that every victim is a part of this secret society." She spat out every word. Her anger coming in barely controlled waves.

Danny and Dr Amiri exchanged a look that I didn't understand, Danny spoke first.

"We do however believe in Alchemy. And we really did find that scroll, that is not a lie. However..." He paused for a moment, looking firmly at Dr Amiri. Who gave a small curt nod of his head, as if giving Danny permission to continue.

"We found the scroll, but we also found another scroll as well, that we kept hidden." He sighed the last, as if defeated.

I could feel my heart racing. Not wanting to stop Danny from saying more I calmly sat there just

looking at him, maintaining a blank expression on my
face.

"When we deciphered the scroll, we found that it was
in fact a letter. Written by Cleopatra herself to an
unknown person. Stating that she would be travelling
across the Indian ocean, to a secret island that she
had been told about. An island which was larger than
any other island.

Located far beyond the red sea."

I stared in disbelief.

"You think that she came here, to escape her fate?"

"Yes, we do. That is why we are going to the glass
house mountains. We think there may be a clue
there." He looked at me, a look passed his face that
read clearly that there was more.

"The letter also tells of a hidden cave made of
gemstones, that lays between the volcanic
mountains." He studied us for a moment, waiting for
our reaction.

"Wow. Just...wow." It's all I could manage to say.

"So, the serpents why do you both have them?" Jules
chimed in, cutting me off from saying any more.

Danny leaned across his knees towards us. Dr Amiri
placed a hand on each of ours. Jules and I reacted at
the same time. We both jerked our hands away. An
expression of hurt crossed his face.

He quickly composed himself sitting up stiffly in his
seat. Clearing his throat before he spoke. smoothing
down his suit jacket, clearly trying to mask the

discomfort he now felt.

"We wear them because through our journey's over the years, we have become quite transfixed, in alchemy and the story behind the Ouroboros. Many connections can be made between the aboriginal tribes of Australia and their rituals of worship. Mirroring those not only throughout the Middle East but more importantly Egypt.

A pyramid stands West of the blue mountains.

"But there aren't any pyramids here in Australia?" I said quite confidently.

"Ah, but there is." Dr Amiri had a twinkle in his eye now and a smug look on his face to match.

He pulled out his smart phone and quickly typed on the touch screen then handed me the phone. On the small screen was an image of a massive mountain, covered in thick vegetation. The mountain was in the perfect shape of a pyramid! "This is called Walsh's pyramid and archaeologists have been debating back and forth for years about the possibility, that beneath 5000 years of soil and plant build up, that there is a pyramid hidden within. Of course, there are many experts in our field who will also argue that it's just not possible. But let's be real here, who are we to depict what is possible or not when giant structures have been erected since early civilizations began, with no concrete evidence as to how.

The bigger question you should be asking is *how* so many ancient civilizations all not only believed in many of the same deities in their own way of worship, but how pyramids of enormous magnitude have been erected all over the world. Without any proof that these civilizations even connected with one another. It's as though something more was connecting them in their faith."

I nodded, as kooky as it sounded it was a valid question, one that I knew had been on archaeologists' minds for centuries.

"So why are we going to the glass house mountains instead of the pyramid?" Jules asked.

"Because we believe that the pyramid is only the power source, not the gateway." replied Danny.

Just then the speaker overhead crackled to life. "We will be taking off in a moment, please ensure that your seat belts are fastened. Thank you."

"I was so swept up in listening to you, that I hadn't even felt the plane moving."

I said as the pilot cut off his speaker connection.

"Neither had I." Replied both Jules and Danny simultaneously. Before he turned back to the window, to watch us take off from the tar mac.

Chapter Eighteen

Dr Amiri stood and walked to the cock pit. He disappeared inside before reappearing a few minutes later.

"We are nearing the mountains now. There is vacant farmland near the base of the mountain. That's where we will land. It's as close to the mountain as we can get. We will have to go the rest of the way on foot." Dr Amiri grabbed his bag and went to the bathroom. "I'm going to change, I suggest all of you prepare for landing, it's going to be rough."

I didn't need to be told twice I grabbed my seat belt. Quickly fastening it tightly around my mid-section. Jules was already ahead of me. We sat quietly waiting for Dr Amiri to return. Being this close to Jules made me feel stronger somehow. As though her very presence made a deep connection inside of me. As though she read my mind, Jules reached her hand out to me, clasping her hand around mine. She gave me a comforting look. "It's going to be ok Soph. We can do this." Just then the plane veered sharply to the left. The glasses rattled inside the cupboards. I gripped Jules' hand tighter as the plane balanced out and slowly tilted downwards. I let out a long breath, I knew we were dropping in altitude. My ears began to feel as though they were blocked. Dr Amiri returned to his seat, quickly putting on his seat belt. "I just got thrown around. I wasn't expecting that."

The plane was almost on the ground now, I could see the grass just metres from the wheels. We hit the ground with a thump. My teeth rattled in my mouth sending the painful vibration through my ears. We slowed abruptly, then came to a halt. "Did I also mention that these jets don't need as much runway to take off and land. Pretty neat huh'." Danny smiled as he said it, a slight gleam in his eye. The door opened to the cock pit, and the pilot got out, then opened the hatch so we could exit. We all got up and walked down the steps. Dr Amiri turned to the pilot. "Stay here for as long as it takes."

"Will do sir, those where my orders." Nodding he then came down the steps to join us.

The air was cool, but warmer than Canberra in comparison. Winter in Queensland sat at around 19 degrees. A heat wave for us and our acclimatised bodies.

I could see the thick bushland in front of us, that lay at the base of Mt Tibberoowuccum.

That stood towering above us in the nearby distance. We made our way forwards towards the bushland. Danny pulled a large folded brush axe from his backpack. He opened it up, making sure it locked into place properly. He walked on ahead, then began hacking at the undergrowth, trying to clear a path. We walked for what felt like hours, bugs flew into our faces every few minutes. Spider webs clung to our arms as we fought our way through dense shrubbery. Up ahead, the sound of running water, caught my attention. I stopped trying to catch my breath. Bending over I rested my hands on my knees. "I need to rest for a minute, we've been walking for hours." Danny turned to both of us. Ok, ten minutes then we keep going."

"Great coz I need to go to the little girl's room." Replied Jules. I nodded in agreement, before following her into the bush to find a sheltered spot. We came to the small creek; the water was crystal clear. Jules knelt down straight away and began splashing her face. "The water is so cold, it's amazing." She said gasping. I dropped to my knees beside her and took a huge scoop in my cupped hands. I put the water to my lips, just as Danny burst through the bushes. "Don't drink the water!" He bellowed. It was too late, the cool water flowed down my dry parched throat. Just then, the world went into a spin. Images flashed in front of my eyes. Suddenly, I was standing in a cavern. Its walls where adorned in millions of crystals. Three trees stood in a circle surrounding a giant crystal that threatened to protrude out of the ceilings opening.

Three figures stood inside the circle. A woman who

was heavily pregnant stood beside two large men, who had their backs turned facing the woman. She let out a cry, as she collapsed backwards, gripping the enormous crystal. The two men held her on either side, as they gently helped her onto the ground. I watched in fascination as the woman gave birth to not one, but two newborn babies. The first child had white wisps of hair, while the second child had thick dark hair. The children's eyes shone. one held piercing green eyes while the other was brilliant blue. The crystal seemed to spring to life, its glow pierced through the cavern. A doorway appeared and in it they placed the babies. The doorway immediately closed, leaving the Gemstone empty once more. The world swam and I was once again back in the rainforest. Danny was leaning over me. Deep concern was apparent on his face.

"That's three visions in one day Sophia." Concern showing in his voice.

"They are getting stronger. More vivid." I replied, my voice was a little shaken.

"Why did you tell us not to drink the water Danny?" Jules asked. A stern forcefulness was in her words. As she stared at Danny, with a look of steel on her face. He looked as though he wanted to flinch but thought better of it.

"Because this mountain is where the tales of the mystical water Vierg'e come from. I didn't know what the water would do to either of you."

He looked embarrassed as he said that last part.
Jules' face softened.
There was a crunching behind us as Dr Amiri came
through the bushes to where we were all crouched
by the stream. "Come on, we must keep moving. It
will be dark soon."
We all stood. Danny helped me too my feet. "I'm
okay." I said, looking into his concerned eyes.
"Okay." He said after a moment. Seemingly satisfied
he turned to follow Jules who now stood patiently
waiting at the top of the embankment.

Chapter Nineteen

Dusk closed in quickly, as the sun set further below the horizon. long shadows where cast down around us, from the towering gum trees. Their thick foliage now acting as a barrier for the fading light. Danny reached inside his backpack. Retrieving three metal L.E.D torches. He passed one to each of us, before retrieving a head torch for himself.

The sound of an owl echoed unexpectedly above us making me jump.

On and on we walked through the dense rainforest. As the full moon rose higher, it's light began to filter down through the trees. The light looked like streaks as it shone down. Penetrating the darkness, that surrounded us on the forest floor below.

The sound of cicadas was deafening as we drew close to the mountains base. Finally, we arrived where we were met with a hard wall of rock, that rose high into the air. Leaning against the hard rock surface, I took a moment to admire the crystal-clear night sky.

The stars shone brightly, above me.

Jules sat on a nearby rock, clearly exhausted. She
shone her torch to a nearby tree. It's thick trunk
looking odd in the surrounding forest. Which from
what I had seen, consisted mainly of tall thin trunked
scribbly gums. I moved forward, towards the tree.
The light seemed to filter differently across its thick
bark. As I walked closer, I could see the light causing a
shimmer effect in the air. I reached out with my hand,
expecting to touch something solid. Just as I thought I
had made contact, my hand disappeared into thin air.
I jumped back with a squeal, clasping my hand to my
chest as though stung. Danny came rushing to my
side. "It's okay Sophia. Quick!" He called to the
others. "We have found the entrance!"
Confused I looked at Danny, who held my hand as
though it were injured. He smiled with a gleam in his
emerald green eyes, before stepping forwards and
disappearing entirely.
Dr Amiri came behind me followed closely by Jules.
"Come, we must hurry. The cavern is on the other
side of this doorway."
He ushered for us to go through first. Jules gave me a
look, that said. 'come on girl, we can do this.' before
she grabbed my hand and pulled me through behind
her.

Chapter Twenty

We walked through the doorway as though it was never really there. When we emerged onto the other side, we stood on a hard rock surface.

Old crumpled leaves littered the floor around our feet. I turned in time, to see Dr Amiri appear out of the smooth stone wall that now stood at our backs. I followed the line of that wall. The smooth rock stopped in an oval shape, as an enormous boarder of crystals covered the walls around the doorway. The minute I saw the crystals I knew I had seen this cavern before.

Moonlight now streamed through the skylight in the caverns surface. Dr Amiri went to stand by Danny as they stood at the outskirts of a circle of trees.

Their backs where both to us, I could see the moonlight reflecting off of their hair.

I gasped.

'It was both of you, in my vision!' I thought as I stood in shock. The same pin pricks of fear began coursing through my body.

Then my vision began to swim. I could feel Jules' arms wrap around me, lowering me to the floor as I collapsed beneath my own body weight. The air shimmered around me, but this time I did not black out.

Ghostly translucent figures appeared. Stepping out as if to separate themselves from Dr Amiri and Danny's bodies.

"Oh my god." Whispered Jules, as she held me in her arms. I knew then, that her touching me had somehow allowed a transfer. My power of sight was now flowing through her. Giving Jules the power to see everything that I was seeing.

The two ghostly figures melded together into one. Swirls of blue and red swam in the mass, like two liquid's that cannot bond together. They merged so closely they almost formed a single colour, before being flung apart once again.

They Remained in a confined space, swirling around each other continuously. A woman appeared from between the trees. She held out her hand to the ghostly figure. It responded by reaching forward to hold her waiting hand. As she led the way inside the circle. She sat on the thick bed of leaves beneath the trees. Leaning backwards, the ghost lent over her. It embraced the woman in its arms, which now appeared to solidify. The hand that was interlocked with the woman's slid down her waist as she lay on the floor.

Reaching the tatters of her skirt he slid his hand slowly up her thigh. The woman's neck arched back, her lips parting slightly.

The ghost kissed the woman and her hands slid over the ghost's body in return. sending the swirls of blue and green to move in different directions.

The fluid parted as if making way for her touch.

The moonlight shone on her body, her skin glowed in response, a deep gold like the sun.

As the ghost slid between the woman's legs, the swirling colours paused. A thick silver glow began to emanate outwards joining together with the golden glow of the woman's power. In a blinding spectacle of light, the two powers intertwined in the power of moonlight.

Jules shifted beside me shielding her eyes from the blinding light. Then without warning, the light faded, and the ghostly figure was gone.

Only the woman remained, now standing alone holding her heavily pregnant belly. A look of tenderness was on her face, as she stroked her swollen stomach.

Danny and Dr Amiri appeared beside her, placing each of their hands on her shoulders.

Danny had an aura of red that surrounded him, and Dr Amiri was a brilliant blue. I realised in that moment that their aura matched the stones they wore, encircled with the Ouroboros. I looked at

Danny's hand as it rested on the woman's shoulder.
Sure, enough a large ruby ring sat in full view. The
moon shone down upon the trio; their skin remained
neutral. There was no otherworldly glow this time.
The woman stepped forward; her hand outstretched
towards us.
We both stood, walking simultaneously towards the
three waiting figures. Jules' hand enclosed around
mine as we reached the circle. I took the woman's
hand. The moment I did I was flooded with broken
images, that I couldn't understand. I felt Jules stiffen
beside me as she too experienced the flood of images
that where now racing through my mind.
I felt my own power rise to the occasion. Wrapping
itself around the images, they finally slowed. My
power clasped them tightly, before slowly releasing
them one by one, to play like unedited parts of a
movie reel inside my head.
The sky was stained red. Drops of ash fluttered in soft
weightless drops around us. We stood in an open
dessert. The matching red ground rose and fell in
mounds around us. The woman sat alone in the
clearing at our feet.
Her clothes were torn, and she was covered in a thick
layer of red dirt. Her face was almost unrecognisable
as she looked up to the sky.
A thick gold choker attached to a chain was clasped
tightly around her neck. Tiny symbols, where etched
into the flat gold surface.

The world melted away around me, before I was once again left standing in the circular room at the top of the mysterious temple like building, I had seen in my vision. The woman was still tied to the bed just as she had been before. Only this time the queen stood over her. Her long deep red hair flowed around her shoulders in a wisp of black smoke. Like another worldly pet, waiting for orders to strike.

The woman showed a strong defiance on her fragile features. And even as she spoke, the force fullness of her own being was clear.

"you will fail Aaleyah. Rest assured, that even if you imprison me you will still fail. My people will never rest until you are destroyed."

"We will see dear child. The loss of an only daughter, will destroy your father."

"Fear crossed the woman's face now. As she watched that black smoke, weave its way forwards, towards her.

The queen turned, walking to the doorway. With her back turned she spoke.

"Your father will only see you die Aamilia. He will never know, where I have imprisoned you. Eternity is a long time for grief, though I doubt it will take that long for him to finally break. Enjoy my temple in the moments you still have."

With that she left the room. My gaze was once again, transfixed on the horror that was about to play out in front of me. The Smoke curled its way inside Aamilia.

I watched on in horror as it flowed through her nose,
mouth and eyes. Until its entire mass was completely
absorbed by her. That was when she screamed. Her
back arching away from the bed as she rose in pain.
I watched as I entered the room, but rather than
being me. I was nothing more than a white and pale
green shadow, that knelt in a wisp of smoke beside
the woman. I watched as she spoke to me, and I
cringed knowing what was going to happen next. As
her face turned once again to the ceiling, screaming
in pure agony. The black smoke rose from within her
body, filling the air above us like a cloud of death. I
had a moment to feel sorry for what Jules was about
to see, before the sea of scarab beetles rained
downwards covering the bed entirely.
The room melted away transporting us once again, to
the circle of trees in the cave.
A woman of great beauty stood beside a golden
sarcophagus. Which dominated the space around the
base of the crystal. Inside the open sarcophagus was
a frail looking man, covered in dirt and scratches,
held in place by another oversized man that
appeared to be a guard of sorts.
A man dressed as an Egyptian priest was standing at
the front of the sarcophagus reading rapidly from a
large bound book. Speaking in a language I couldn't
understand. The moon consumed the crystal now
sending a great white light emanating through the
sky light towards the heavens. The priest drew blood

from the man's wrist, the knife making a clean cut
against his skin in one quick slash.
The priest rubbed it over the face of the stone.
Leaving a trail of thick red blood, illuminated on the
surface. Still the slave did not take his heavy gaze
from the woman. The woman only flinched as the
priest lunged forwards, stabbing a large jagged knife
into the frail man's chest. He went limp and fell
forwards, into the sarcophagus as the priest slid the
now heavily blood-soaked dagger from his heart.
I watched as the world seemed to slow and time
itself weighed down around us. Turning the air into a
thick almost lead like substance. The circle of trees
grew, their branches intertwining into a barrier
around the small gathered party. The woman spoke
rapidly to the large guard, sending him thumping his
heavy mass across the cave to retrieve a heavy
golden chest. Emblazoned with the same wings of
Osiris that I had seen carved into the foot of the
temple bed. She pressed her hand to the lid of the
box and a soft click echoed gently through the
cavern. Opening the box, a look of pleasure crept up
her face. Her hand disappeared inside the box before
she lifted out a heavy necklace, adorned with the
most brilliant gemstones I had ever bore witness to in
my life. The priest helped her to secure the heavy
gold amulet around her neck before returning to
where he stood, chanting once again from the book.
The woman gestured for another man to come to her.

A frail man scurried towards the woman carrying a woven basket, which he placed gently at her feet before scurrying fearfully away.

She reached inside the basket and produced a hissing snake from within. Placing the snake against her breast she waited patiently for it to pierce her with its fangs. It reared its head back more than happy to attack. As it struck her with a killing force. As the woman collapsed to her knees, trying flimsily to put the snake back into the basket and failing. A large crack emanated through the cavern in a deafening chorus as the snake slithered away into the outskirts of the cave.

From deep within the crystal a figure appeared, his face hidden by the rapidly rising smoke like fog, that now pushed outwards consuming the cave in thick waves.

His voice boomed like a tidal wave through the cavern.

In an ear deafening bass like voice, that held a power all of its own. "Queen Cleopatra, you have done us a great service in freeing us with your mortal magic." The Queen now lay crumpled on her side unable to move, presumably from the snake venom that now ravaged her body. A second figure appeared, striding forwards she laid a gentle hand on the man's shoulder. He bowed to her slightly stepping back to allow her to pass him.

She walked to the dying woman before kneeling on

the cold floor in front of her. She cradled her in her arms as she lifted her limp body from the ground where she lay. A third figure appeared and walked purposefully towards the others. I gasped as I stared at Danny, who was now helping Princess Aamilah to hold Queen Cleopatra. Silence filled the cave as the fog parted and a ghostly figure rose from within the now dead body of Cleopatra. Floating skywards into the silver moonlight before travelling up the channel of light into the heavens above. From out of the clearing fog, stepped Dr Amiri. The three now stood together in a picturesque moment. Amiri's features mirrored that of Aamilah two Fey twins stood proudly in the cave. Danny held Aamilah in a gesture of warmth, as the love they shared flowed out towards Jules and I in a painful emotional blast. That caught my stomach in my throat, as I fought to hold back tears. I savoured the sight in front of me before the world melted away around us, delivering us once again to another time. Aamilah was on the ground, her belly shone as though it held a light all of its own. Amiri and Danny where on either side of her legs. Working together, to help her deliver their child. She gave one final push and Amiri stood. A beautiful baby lay screaming in his arms. He took a shuddery step before kneeling beside Aamilia. Placing the baby on her naked chest. She looked down lovingly at the small baby. Sweat streamed across her brow, and she gripped Amiri with her free hand as she pushed through another contraction. Amiri turned to Danny, a look of shock on his face. Danny knelt forward and lifted a second screaming baby from between Aamilah's legs. He crawled scrapping his knees against the dirt floor to rest the second baby in Aamilah's arms. Looking at the two twins, lying safely in their mothers loving arms I knew in that moment exactly who we were.

The image faded, leaving us standing together once again in the present. I looked at Jules, she was crying silent tears. I squeezed her hand. For the first time in my entire life, something made sense.

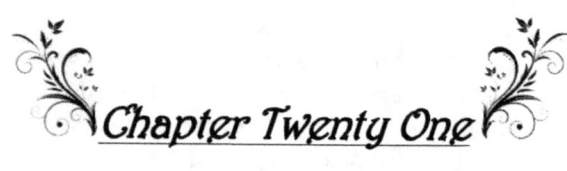

Chapter Twenty One

Farez Amiri walked forward, embracing me tightly in his arms. "I couldn't tell you Sophie, I had to keep you safe. If she knew about the two of you. God, I don't want to think what she would do."

I pulled back from him, enough to stare into his solemn eyes.

"I know. I wouldn't have believed you if you had have told me anyway." He nodded, a little too rapidly, then turning his head slightly he wiped away tears.

"Sorry to break up the love fest guys, but how are we supposed to go up against the queen!" Jules interrupted.

"You don't have to my child." A cold clear voice echoed across the cave. Sending a chill down to my core. I knew without turning, that the owner of that voice would be behind me, sure enough she was.

Her skin was a deep olive, that glowed slightly with her power. Her hair flowed around her like a sea of smoke. As she spoke, the smoke seemed to pull back with every word as if afraid of her. Which now slowly

expanded through the room. an icy cold hand ran
through the air as if searching its surroundings.

It stopped abruptly like a shimmering line in front of
where Jules and I stood. Unable to touch either of us.
It hung there patiently waiting.

The Queen walked towards us, her hair billowing
behind her as though her own aura created a silent
wind.

"Danus my son, how good of you to bring me to this
little party. Where it not for your loyalty, I may not be
here to witness the greatest moment in the history of
our kind." She stared at Danny, with a gaze like ice. I
bet many people had bowed down to her over the
ages, just from that look alone.

Danny shifted uncomfortably under her stare.

It was Amiri who spoke first. "You fool!" He spat at
Danny. His skin began to glow a fierce blue. Danny
stepped back, preparing for a fight. He responded
with his own power flaring to life in a shimmer of red.

"*STOP!*" Yelled Aamilah. The power slowly faded from
both the men. Even as they stood apart, the promise
of a fight still hung in the air.

Clapping sounded, as the Queen walked between
them applauding them both and smiling.

"Now, now. There will be plenty of time for fighting
before the night draws to a close."

"Please Queen Aaleyah, we don't have to do this."
And even though her voice sounded firm, Sophie
knew that a part of Aamilah had already given up.

The queen turned to Aamilah; her smile gone.
Replaced by a look of pity.
"Juliana, come to me my child. Look upon your
mother's face and tell me truthfully.
Is she everything you hoped and dreamed that she
would be?" Jules gripped my hand but refused to
answer her. The queen turned her attention onto
Jules and I. 'Not good, not good.' I kept repeating
over and over in my head. As she strode towards us
looking angry.
"Your defiance can only get you so far my dear.
Sooner or later you will do as I ask, whether you are
willing or not."
"What is she talking about?" Jules asked to whoever
was willing to answer.
Danny sighed, a deep tired sigh that slumped his
shoulders forward.
"She wants you to become the one. To become the
key that will open the veil that divides the worlds.
Which in turn will once again allow the Djinn to roam
freely across your world."
He couldn't bring himself to look up as he spoke.
Choosing instead to stare at the ground the entire
time.
"You have two choices, either you can do this
willingly, or I can force you. Either way this will
happen and now. No more stalling, the moon is
almost upon us!" The queen gestured at the sky light
then stared intently at Jules.

Jules looked at Amiri. "And if I refuse."

"Then she will force you, and that will be more painful than you could ever possibly imagine."

"Now hurry up and sacrifice the prisoner, time is drawing down on us." She waved nonchalantly in Sophie's direction with a voice that sounded bored.

"We can't, it's not that simple." Said Danny, as he walked towards us. The queen looked at him, her eyes narrowing. "What are you up to Danus?" Questioned the queen, her suspicion was now quickly turning into a look of anger.

"She is your granddaughter, mother dear." He spat the last words with a feeling of deep bitterness in his voice.

"Well played Danus, well played. A double agent. Well I'm glad that you learnt something over the years." The queen stood staring at Danny with a look of pure hatred.

"Oh' what's wrong Aaleyah, didn't you know. That's too bad." He pretended to pout like a child before a smile crept over his lips.

The queen looked like she had swallowed a fly. Disgust was clear on her face.

"You see mother, I wanted you here. In this exact moment. Nothing gives me more pleasure than seeing the look on your face when you fail. Again." Danny was standing beside Jules now. He looked at her and let his pain show on his face.

"Jules I'm so sorry." Danny reached out to comfort

her, but his attention was quickly drawn back to the Queen.

"How dare you, and after all I have sacrificed!" She thrust her power outward towards us Danny tried to react, but he was too slow. I was flung backwards slamming into the wall behind me. The gemstones sticking into my flesh like tiny blades of shattered glass. I cried in pain falling forwards onto my knees. I felt the first trickle of blood run down my back. Jules collapsed to the floor beside me in despair.

"Please. No, there has to be another way." Jules was on her knees, begging. Her head hung down; her hands now swung loosely at her sides.

I pulled myself up from the ground, the pain shot through my back sharply. Making me catch my breath, as I forced myself to kneel in front of Jules. Gently cupping her chin in my hands.

She slowly turned her head up, now facing me with tear ridden eyes. Fresh tears trickled down my thumbs, weaving their way around my wrists as I looked deep into her eyes."It's okay Jules." I whispered to her, just inches from her face. I smiled at her. My beloved sister, who was always stronger than me. Who now sat defeated, raw emotion spilling between us.

"Do you trust me Jules?" She nodded rapidly. I willed my power to rise as I sent images of what I had gathered from my visions. The image I had received containing the details of the binding of Amiri and

Danus flowed into Jules' mind. Fresh tears welled in her eyes.

"I want this. You have a place in this world Jules. I have never been a part of it, not really anyway." Her eyes widened.

"It's suicide Soph!" She exclaimed, with fresh tears tumbling from her eyes. She reached her hands upwards, now clasping mine.

Looking deep into her eyes I willed her to see what I was feeling. The feeling of power pulled at us along that invisible line. Connecting us together, in a way it felt so right. As though this was our destiny. In that moment, feeling our shared power flowing together in unison. We both came to a realisation. That in a way, we had always been two halves of a whole, and by binding ourselves together we were completing that missing piece of one another.

I knew then that Jules understood completely that rather than me giving up and surrendering myself. I was giving myself over to our one true self. I knew deep down that just as Amiri and Danny had been bound together when they created us. That if they could be separated again, that so could we. But first we had business to take care of. And that meant defeating the evil queen of the west.

We both knew that this was the only way. 'I love you, and I will find a way to bring you back I promise.' Jules' words sung softly in my head.

'I know.' I replied as the power retreated back along

that invisible line. She moved my hands away from her face. Then wiping the tears from her eyes, she stood. I knew in that moment, that nothing could stand in her way. Something inside of her had changed. I had never thought it possible until this very moment to see my sister as my protector and yet here we are staring death in the face and for once, I wasn't afraid to admit that I was petrified.

Chapter Twenty-two

"What will happen if I allow you to pull forth my powers?" She asked with a new feeling of strength, projecting from her.

I realised that even though we were no longer touching, that Jules and I could still feel each other through the invisible string that held us together. Jules must have sensed it too because she looked at me.

A look of concern was plain on her face, I didn't need to be connected to her to know what she was thinking.

'Nothing. Nothing will happen at all.'

I thought really hard about that for a moment.

Jules nodded. She had heard my thought, seen what I was thinking in that moment we had just shared. The million-dollar question was, did the queen know.

I flicked my attention to her. She seemed to flinch slightly at the sudden attention, that I was now giving to her. As quickly as it came, it went. Almost as if it was never there at all. But I had seen it, she was afraid.

The big scary queen of the Djinn was scared, because deep down inside she didn't know what was going to happen. Her vision of what should happen, blinded her from any other reasoning or rational thought.

All she knew, was that Jules was the key. She had betted on that since the day she found out Jules had been born.

What she hadn't planned on was that I was also a part of that equation. Now her perfectly mapped out plan was hitting a snag, with the potential to crumble around her. And she was scared.

'We must act quickly, while there is still time!' I thrust the thought into Jules as hard as I could. Jules looked sternly at me; she had heard.

She clasped her hands around my wrists tightly, I instantly felt the heat of her power. I responded willingly, opening my own power up to her and letting it flow out to meet hers. The power entwined as it instantly recognised its other half.

Blinding purple light now surrounded us as we held each other. It was an intimacy that had no words to describe it. I felt a doorway open in my mind; I didn't hesitate. I flew towards the waiting door letting my subconscious go within.

Jules' voice flowed through me as if filling every spare space in my mind. She gave me thoughts of love, and protection and warmth. In that moment I knew, that no matter what happened, Jules would protect me for all of eternity. I trusted her completely, after all she was my other half. Together we would be the most powerful deity, the worlds had ever seen.

The light faded as I looked down at my now empty hands. 'Jules, it's ok I'm here.'

I breathed a sigh of relief, hearing Sophie's voice ring through my head. 'Jules, focus. Use your smokeless fire. Banish her back into the other realm. We must hurry, the moon is in perfect alignment. If we don't act now, then the veil between the worlds will be open forever.'

I turned slowly, to stare at the cracked crystal shard that now lay glowing in the light of the moon.

I wanted to touch it. Just a thought and I was there. I felt more alive than I had ever felt in my life. My skin tingled with the sensation of the world around me. I glanced lazily at the faces in the room, I could see clearly now. The world seemed to make more sense. The queen stood on the far side of the cave. Her Djinn clinging to her empty vessel of a body. Danus, stood to my right beside Amiri and Aamilia. His Djinn flowed through his core fighting to get out. Amiri stood like a pillar of light, besides his sister. Their heavenly glow beamed softly from within their shells. I rested my hand against the cold flat surface of the crystal. Instantly, the power of the convergence came into me. I could see the stars, as I felt the weight of a thousand eons fighting to flow through my soul. I glanced back at the Queen, she stood motionless, patiently waiting with a look of pleasure on her face.

She thinks I am doing this for her. She believes that what she is seeing is supposed to happen. I felt anger burn inside me, as an unpleasant thought came to me.

Without thinking of whether it was even possible, I called to her Djinn. Willed it to separate itself and come to its true master.

It responded willingly, much to the queen's horror. It tore itself from around her soul, ripping at its bonds as it fought its way from within her body. Claws protruded from her chest as they pierced through her pale skin. A heavy sucking sound echoed throughout the cave as the Djinn made a hole wide enough to escape. It came to me, projecting a feeling of remorse. I ignored its plea, just as it had ignored the plea of all the innocent lives it had killed in its search for power.

I channelled the energy of the convergence that now swelled within me. Creating a portal within the last sliver of light from the moon. I thrust the Djinn through the portal into the waiting blackness beyond. Then closing the doorway with nothing more than a thought, I turned to the waiting faces of my family. Princess Aamilah walked fearlessly to me and wrapped her arms around me tightly. Placing a gentle kiss on my cheek and whispering thank you in my ear. I felt the magic soften, retreating back to within its little box inside of me. I released a heavy breath that I didn't know that I was holding, Danny and Amiri came to me and held us both in an embrace. It would take a little getting used to thinking of them all as my family but having the visions in my mind of our shared past helped to bridge that gap. Sophia was still alive I could feel her presence swell within me and a strong feeling of pride rise up. An emotion that was not my own doing. Yes, this is definitely going to take some getting used to.

"With all this shared power residing inside me. What if I turn evil like the Queen?" I asked looking over at her bloody body, that lay like a piece of discarded meat on the cave floor. Aamilah touched my cheek gently, pulling my gaze from the bloody remains, to stare into her emerald green eyes.

"You have much to learn my beautiful child, but you will. With our help you will." She looked at Amiri and Danny as she spoke the last. Danny chimed in.

"As long as Sophia is within you, your shared power will remain in perfect balance. Her consciousness will not only help you to remain humble but also alleviate any shortcomings you are likely to face in the future." He looked at Amiri with a look of compassion. Amiri replied heartily.

"Of course, we can share our wisdom with you too. As sharing a consciousness is quite the learning curve to say the least."

I gave a weak smile. "Thank you." I replied taking a moment to give them the full weight of my gratitude into the smile as I could gather. It was a human gesture, to be sure. One that I hoped I could still hold onto for a while longer now that Sophia and I had become a deity of sorts. "What does this mean, for us all now?" I asked hoping someone had the answer. "Well I don't know about you but I for one have been running, fighting, hiding and been imprisoned for thousands of years. Not to mention trapped in a body with this guy in amongst all that. I could use a break." He

jerked a thumb in Danny's direction in jest. 'Did he just make a joke? No freaking way!' I heard Sophie's shock emanate through me. I burst into laughter I couldn't help it; it was so unexpected the three actually jumped with surprise. Before we all were laughing uncontrollably, with a mixture of relief, pent up anxiety and exhaustion.

Aamilah was the first to break the chorus of infectious laughter.

"Let us go home and announce to our people what has happened. We will have a feast in Juliana and Sophia's honour. Unfortunately, we will have to take her with us as proof." She pointed a finger at the queens remains and shivered in disgust.

"Let me take care of it." Danny used his magic to lift shroud the queen in his smokeless fire and lift her from the ground, levitating her in the air.

Aamilah held my hand and using her magic channelled an image of her home in the forest realm. I reached within myself and willed my magic to assist with making a portal to transport us through the veil. It appeared in front of us and I allowed Aamilah to guide me through to the other side. Danny and Amiri crossed through behind us and I immediately closed the portal. I stood in awe as we gathered in the lush green forest of the Fey realm. I could feel the trees whispering our names through the forest in excited conversations, I knew in that moment that we were finally home.

To be continued...

Book 2
Imperium
January 2021